CW01099863

## About the Author

A presenter, comedian, actor and DJ, Ryan is a born entertainer.

If he's not hosting features for BBC's *The One Show*, he's raving behind the decks or telling jokes on stage.

It all started in BBC Northern Ireland, where Ryan landed his first 'real' job as a TV runner in 2008.

Fast forward a few years later and the funnyman found himself warming up audiences on ITV's *Loose Women*.

Not long after heading for the bright lights of London, Hand got his big break; presenting Saturday night TV on ITV's *Cannonball*.

The rest, as they say, is history.

Now a published author, the proud Irishman has added yet another string to his bow, though he's always been an avid writer.

Penning stories as a kid, poems and songs as a teenager and now books as a full-fledged grown up, Ryan has always enjoyed escaping within his own imagination.

STARDUST
AMAZING ARCHIE THE SINGING
SENSATION

Ryan Hand

# STARDUST
# AMAZING ARCHIE THE SINGING
# SENSATION

Pegasus

PEGASUS PAPERBACK

© Copyright 2023
**Ryan Hand**

The right of Ryan Hand to be identified as author of
this work has been asserted by him in accordance with the
Copyright, Designs and Patents Act 1988

**All Rights Reserved**

No reproduction, copy or transmission of this publication
may be made without written permission.
No paragraph of this publication may be reproduced,
copied or transmitted save with the written permission of the
publisher, or in accordance with the provisions
of the Copyright Act 1956 (as amended).

Any person who does any unauthorised act in relation to
this publication may be liable to criminal
prosecution and civil claims for damage.

A CIP catalogue record for this title is
available from the British Library

ISBN-978-1-91090-382-7

*Pegasus is an imprint of
Pegasus Elliot MacKenzie Publishers Ltd.*
www.pegasuspublishers.com

First Published in 2023

**Pegasus
Sheraton House Castle Park
Cambridge CB3 0AX England**

Printed & Bound in Great Britain

To my mum Pauline, who made me shoot for the stars.
This one's for you mother bear x

Thanks to Emma Douglas for the wonderful artwork and illustration of Archie, and to Ryan Harty for designing and styling the front cover.

The amazing mentors I've come across along my way: English teachers, media tutors and work colleagues; thanks for making it a fun journey so far.

To my family and friends who've always believed in me and my dreams, thanks for always having my back.

Remember, if you can dream it, you can do it.
Anything is possible.

# Prologue

How did Spiderman become a web-slinging superhero? How did Mary Poppins learn to look after naughty children? How did Archie Mills become a singing sensation?

"Who's Archie Mills?"

Wait, you don't know Archie Mills? Amazing Archie the Singing Sensation?

I'm Archie Mills...

Perfectly normal, with normal friends and a normal life. I'm your everyday, average kinda kid.

Well, I 'was' perfectly normal and then *BOOM*, my life changed forever.

Ever heard of stardust? No? Neither had I.

It's like magic, but better.

Turns out, we've all got a little bit of stardust inside each and every one of us. But if you don't use your stardust, you'll never know what could've been.
So sit back, relax and let me tell you how your wildest dreams can come true...

# Chapter 1

First, let's start with the basics, the nuts and bolts. My name is Archie Mills, I'm thirteen and I live in Wandsworth Town in London. My house is exactly 5.5 miles away from Big Ben.

Did you know Big Ben was originally named The Great Bell, but if you think about it, what's so great about a bell? I guess that's why they called it Big Ben. I suppose they could've called it anything really, Tall Tim, Huge Harry… Massive Mick.

Anyway, I live with my mum and dad at 143 Oakhill Road. Weirdly, every house on my street is painted a different colour. Our house is baby blue, our neighbours' house is bright pink and the people next to them live in a zingy yellow coloured house.

Mum is a dinner lady at my old Primary School (which obviously has its perks). Whatever the schoolkids don't eat gets brought home to Oakhill Road. Shortbread, chocolate sponge cake, strawberry jelly; you name it, we get it.

Dad is an accountant. He works in a skyscraper in London City Centre for Mr Mountgammy, the CEO of Mountgammy Money Limited. Mr Mountgammy is old and grey but really friendly and generous. He always says, "You can work here when you're eighteen, son, just like your dad."

You see some people paint pictures, write poems or create music, but me, I like numbers. My brain is a human calculator. I live for numeracy; decimal points, percentages, multiplication, Pythagoras theorem, LONG DIVISION — now we're talking!

My dad wants me to follow in his footsteps and become an accountant, but I'm only thirteen, I have my whole life to decide what I want to be. The world is my oyster!

The only other thing I've ever wanted to become is a footballer. Imagine having eighty thousand football fans chanting your name; "Archie, Archie, Archie", or whatever your name might be.

Smashing the ball from thirty yards into the top right hand corner of the net to clinch victory in the dying embers of the game, that'd be wicked.

So, that's the long and short of it. A brief introduction. For now, you pretty much know the basics.

At this moment in time, I'm a perfectly normal, everyday thirteen-year-old kid. But I probably should warn you that my life is about to change pretty darn quickly.

So buckle up, because we're in for one helluva ride...

# Chapter 2

We've all got that one crazy best friend; mine is Izzy Jones. Izzy wears daisy chains, tie dye t-shirts and does yoga ten times a day. She has frizzy, bouncy, blonde curly hair and she's the happiest, most positive person I know. You can hear Izzy's laugh from a mile away. She makes everything in life that little bit rosier.

Every day with Izzy is an adventure, but Fridays are always the same, because on Fridays we go to Borough Market. Oh, beautiful Borough Market, aka food heaven. Cuisine from all over the world served from tiny little stalls nestled under the train tracks of London Bridge.

They've got it all; sushi from Japan, Pad Thai from Thailand, paella from Spain, jumbo hotdogs from Germany, smelly cheese from France, Dutch mini-pancakes and sumptuous Swiss chocolate. Every time I go, the smell wafts right up my nostrils and my tastebuds perk up like the spikes on a hedgehog's back.

Izzy's mum is also a dinner lady and I think that's why we both love food so much. Our parents have taken us to Borough Market every Friday since we were babies. But this is the first Friday that we've been allowed to come alone. It's the first Friday of the summer holidays, and it's also Izzy's thirteenth birthday, which can only mean one thing.

We're both officially teenagers!

"Look at us, Archie, riding the train to Borough Market, in charge of our own pocket money and making grown-up decisions all by ourselves. Nothing to see here, guys, just a couple of kids becoming adults," gloats Izzy.

"Adults; independent, responsible adults, that's exactly what we are, Izzy... Until five p.m. of course, when we have to meet Dad at the station. But until then, we're adults."

Everything about this journey feels different than before. The softness of our seats, the squeaking of the train against the tracks, the smell of the carriage. I'm seeing, hearing and feeling it all in vivid, technicolour surround sound, and it feels good.

"Next stop, London Bridge!"

The train announcer signals that we've arrived, and boy do we know it! The curved arched glass roof of Borough Market twinkles in front of our very eyes. We rush down the steps of the station to be greeted by the hustle and bustle of the marketplace. Greengrocers, bread makers, fishmongers and florists, all yelling out and trying to lure in customers with bargain busting deals and free samples.

"Jellied eels, anyone? Get your slippery, slidey, shaky water snakes right here, fresh out of the Thames," shouts a big, burly, Cockney market trader.

"OK, as it's my birthday, I'm going straight to the velvet cupcake stand. And then after that, we can go straight to Percy's Rags, Borough's most famous second-hand shop. It's just round the corner. You can help me pick a birthday jacket."

"Izzy, why would anyone want to go second-hand shopping when they could go first-hand shopping? Why buy something musty and dusty that's already been worn by someone else? Especially on your birthday!"

"Well, Archie, the environment, global warming, recycling, giving a once-cherished item of clothing a new home... I can go on for longer if I really must. Plus, vintage clothing is cool."

To be fair, Izzy makes a valid point.

"Look, Archie, Nero's of Napoli has moved right next to the cupcake stand. It's your favourite."

"Looks like we're about to kill two birds with one stone."

Now, I don't know about you guys, but I think Fridays should start with a supersized slice of pepperoni pizza. I could eat pizza till the cows come home. The cheesier the better, and today it looks extra cheesy.

"A slice of your gooeyist, cheesiest pizza, please, Nero!"

14

Nero hands over a slice and it's piping hot, hotter than molten lava and fresh out the oven.

**\*OUCH\***

The only downside of eating piping hot pizza, is when it burns the arch of your mouth. Yep, you guessed it, that just happened!

"I've got an idea, how about I stuff my face with this deliciously velvety smooth cupcake, and you walk with your mouth wide open. By the time we get to Percy's, the cold air will have cooled the burning sensation right down. You'll be good as new Archie," assures Izzy.

*\*AHHH\**

*\*URGH\**

OK then, Percy's it is…

# Chapter 3

***TRINGGGG***

Sounds the bell at the entrance of Percy's.

"Looking for anything in particular, young man?" shrieks a voice from behind a long glass counter.

'The exit door' is the first thing that springs to my mind, but I smile politely and nod.

"Nope, I'm just here with my best friend Izzy, whose head is now buried in that big mountain of coats over there."

This must be Percy; a tall, pale, middle-aged man who's wearing a waistcoat and a feathered headpiece. He has silver jewellery dangling from every inch of his body, and a striking jet-black goatee beard long enough to land a plane on.

"Excellent. Well, in that case, I'll just go ahead and pop on some music then," grinned Percy.

*Great, and while you're at it, you should spray some air freshener, this place reeks.* Obviously, I don't say this aloud, but it sure does smell fusty in here.

Percy pulls a vinyl record from its cover and gently slips it onto the vintage record player that sits on top of his glass counter. He lifts the needle and places it into the grooves of the vinyl record. Faint music begins to crackle in the background.

"Ooh, c'mon, Archie, this is the most fun shop in all of London. Look at all the costumes we can play with. Don't be such a prude! You know you really should think about joining me and invest in some high-quality second-hand clothing."

*Uh oh! This sounds like trouble; Izzy's wacky ideas usually don't end well.*

She taps her fingers off her chin, and scans the shop while looking devilishly mischievous.

"Hmm, how about... this cowboy hat? Howdy partner, fancy a trip to the Wild West?"

Izzy pretends to be a cowgirl pulling imaginary guns from her imaginary holsters.

"Or how about... becoming a scuba diver in this wetsuit! It'll keep you dry if it rains!"

"If I go home and tell Mum I spent my hard-earned pocket money on a wetsuit, I'll end up in hot water."

"OK, I see where we're going with this... He doesn't like the hat, nor does he like the wetsuit, so let's look for something more sophisticated. Something smart and snazzy, like... that purple furry coat."

"Yeah, that'd be great, if I wanted to dress up as a woolly mammoth."

"Don't be such a bore, Archie, it's my birthday. Try it on, it'll be fun, you'll look cool."

"Oh OK, what's the worst that can happen…" I mutter into myself.

Those were the words that changed my life forever.

My advice to you is never ever say those words, because nine times out of ten, something usually DOES happen.

As soon as I slip my arm into the sleeve of the purple furry coat, I instantly start to feel all warm and fuzzy. I feel tingly, like a billion Skittles have just exploded inside my body. It's as if electric atoms are swishing around my bloodstream like bumper cars knocking into one another. I feel like I'm sliding down a giant rainbow. And this is when it happened for the very first time…

*"A boom, boom, boom*
*A shake, a little boogie*
*A click of my feet,*
*And I start to feel groovy,*
*A dibbidy doo,*
*A slip and a slide,*
*I found my new voice,*
*And I'm singing inside,*
*A hip and a hop,*
*I'm feeling on top,*
*I'll dance in my pants,*
*I ain't gonna stop…"*

Izzy looks at me gobsmacked, as if I've just turned into a unicorn. "Holy cow, what the hell was that?"

She's not the only one dumbfounded and baffled; ten strangers are now also gawking through Percy's shop window too.

Percy's jaw is practically lying on the till, which is strange because he looks like the type of man who eats dictionaries for breakfast, and even he can't find the words.

"I... I... I'm, speech... less."

*WOW! Did I just do that?*

In my tender thirteen years of life, I've never sang a single song, *NEVER!* I can't sing, I can't dance, I'm the son of an accountant who likes numbers and football. The coat, it's the coat, it must be magic, but these guys don't know that...

Izzy pipes up, "Earth to Archie, do you realise what just happened?"

If truth be told, I'm a little dazed, I know what happened, I just don't know how...

"I'll take it!"

I slam a £20 note onto Percy's glass counter. Percy looks like he's just seen a ghost. He quickly packs the coat into a brown paper bag, handing it over nervously.

"Here, it's yours," frets Percy.

In situations like this, I always find it's best to have an escape plan, so I shoot out the door like a horse bolting from its stable.

"MATE, where are you going, come back!"

Izzy runs after me, giving chase as we weave in and out of the human traffic that descends on Borough Market. We narrowly dodge people as I sprint with my bag towards London Bridge. It feels like I've just invented fire, like I've inherited some kind of crazy super power. My hand and arm carrying the bag is pulsating, as if possessed by a demon.

"Archie, slow down! Archie!"

# Chapter 4

*AH... AH... AHH\**

"Oy! Speedy Gonzales, what was all that about back there?" demands Izzy with her arms folded, clearly not impressed.

I'm huffing and puffing and lying on the ground outside London Bridge Station. Izzy towers over me, looking for answers. I've never been so out of breath in all my life, I can barely reply.

Luckily for me, I can see the station clock and it's 4:59 p.m. Dad is due around the corner any second now...

"Archie! The song you just sang in Percy's, I never knew you could..."

"Dad, over here!" I shout in giddy, desperate excitement.

*PHEW!* Never have I been as glad to see my old man in all my life.

"Kids, you're on time? I'm shocked! I thought I'd need a police search party to find you. C'mon let's head for the train and beat the rush, then you can tell me all about your day."

Dad is happy to see us and I'm happy to see him. His arrival is a temporary smokescreen that buys me some time before Izzy starts to ask any more questions about my impromptu performance in Percy's.

As we board the train Dad makes awkward small-talk conversation, which Izzy blatantly ignores, as she continues to eyeball me from across the carriage. Her pupils are silently prodding for answers and burning into the back of my head.

"What's in the bag? Did you buy Izzy a birthday present?"

Oh uh! Now Dad's onto me too… I'll have to make something up! GOT IT!

Sometimes in life, you have to tell a little white lie. Now let's be clear here — lying isn't big and it's not clever! Apparently, your nose grows by a centimetre with every lie you tell, but where a magic jacket is concerned, needs must.

"It's… for my history project." I squirm sheepishly.

Dad's eyebrows zip upwards towards the sky, he isn't buying my phony excuse, immediately butting in with his reply, "But school's out for the summer!"

*Darn it, think on your feet, Archie, say something smart, ingenious and unrepliable.*

"Well, Dad… this year, I'm going to be more prepared than ever. You know what they say, right, 'If you fail to prepare, prepare to fail'."

Dad's eyebrows arch back downwards, he looks impressed by my philosophical out-of-the-blue retort. He sits back in his seat, gives it a minute's thought then picks up his paper before beginning to read. And just like that, I'm off the hook.

As the train slowly trundles home, I can feel the aura and magnetism of the jacket coming from inside the bag — it feels alive!

We make it back to Wandsworth Town and drop Izzy off first. This certainly has been a birthday to remember...for both of us.

"Bye, mate, enjoy the rest of your day," I hoot while skipping off merrily with Dad.

Izzy waves from her front garden, standing with a bemused look across her face. Thankfully that's the end of her questions, for now.

Finally, Dad and I arrive home. I burst through the front door, race up the stairs, slamming my bedroom door shut behind me. I calmly set the bag on my bed, not wanting to cause any sudden movements or damage to the contents inside.

"Archie, aren't you going to come down and tell me all about your day at Borough Market?" shouts Mum from the bottom of the stairs.

"I'll be down in a minute!"

Quite frankly, I haven't got time to talk about my day, I've got more pressing matters to deal with.

I take a few paces back from the edge of my bed, gently resting my phone on the shelf of my bedroom wall. I prop the phone against my collection of football sticker books and press record on the video. If it's true, if the jacket is magic, I need to see it with my very own eyes.

I need to film it!

As I take the coat from Percy's paper bag, a golden ray of light illuminates from inside.

Easy tiger, nice and easy does the trick.

I slowly slip my arm into the same sleeve that I first entered and just like that, it happens again.

*"Shoot, shoot, shoot for the sky,*
*I'm a rocket man, baby, and I'll tell you why*
*And yes, yes, yes you can,*
*Believe in yourself, it's a hell of a plan,*
*Spread your wings,*
*Let's see what it brings,*
*Like an eagle so high,*
*Let me see you fly."*

*Ahhhhh!*

I don't even need to watch the video back to realise what just happened. The coat is magic!

Every time I wear it, I become some sort of rock and roll star, but how?

I sit on my bed trying to work out the equation while the coat hangs from the wardrobe door in front of me.

I've been staring at it for nearly an hour now, thinking of all the reasons why this happens.

Maybe it'll talk to me... Maybe there are some clues in the coat's pockets.

Damn. Nothing, nada, zilch, but wait.

On the inside of the coat, there's a name tag, it says:

*'Property of Blue Davies'*

Who's Blue Davies?

If there's one person who will know, it's the Internet. Not that the Internet is a real person, but you know what I mean. OK, I tap on my computer keyboard and search *'Who is Blue Davies?'*

And so it reads:

*'Blue Davies was a famous American soul singer who made his name in Las Vegas performing throughout the 1960s.'*

Wait a minute! This coat belongs to a musical legend? How on earth did it end up in London? More than five thousand miles away from Vegas! And how is it now hanging from my wardrobe door in Wandsworth Town?

*'View Images'*

***CLICK***

WOW, this guy was mega famous. There he is photographed with the King of Rock 'n' Roll, and laughing with that beautiful Hollywood actress Marilyn.

OK, this is crazy, it's all a little too crazy. And sometimes, when things get too crazy in life, you just need to lie down. Lie down and close your eyes and take a deep breath for a minute or two. That's right, take a deep breath, just like that. Breathe in, annnd breathe out... Breathe innnn... and

*Zzzzzz*

*Zzzzzzz*

# Chapter 5

"Hellooo, wakey wakey, Mr Mills!"

"Mr Archie Mills… I bring to you a cup of Wandsworth's finest coffee and a pain au chocolat fresh from Pierre's Pastries."

*HUH! Am I dreaming? That sounds like Izzy's voice trapped inside my head.*

NO! It's not a dream! It's Saturday morning! I'm lying on top of my bed and it *is* Izzy's actual voice. She's howling through my letterbox.

I've somehow fallen asleep and managed to snooze right through. It's light outside, I didn't even pull my curtains or go down for dinner… I didn't even change into my PJs.

***\*ARRHHHH\****

I stretch like a sprawled-out cat and rub the sleep from my eyes. That's better.

Usually, Izzy would be halfway up the stairs by now, but on Saturday mornings, Mum goes shopping and Dad plays golf, so I'll have to let her in myself.

***\*THUD\****
***\*THUD\****
***\*THUD\****

Down the stairs I go, I stomp my way to the bottom step, turn the doorknob and…

"Crikey! You look like you've slept in yesterday's clothes!"

"Yes, Izzy, I have, thanks for noticing. And clearly you don't need to go to the optician's anytime soon, what very observant eyes you have."

"Well, this should kickstart your engine. A latte with a splash of almond milk and a pastry from Pierre. He said '*Bonjour, Mademoiselle* Izzy, where is Mr Archie?' but in a cute French accent"

"A wake-up call and breakfast, thanks Izzy."

***SLURRRPP****

*Mmm, that sure is good coffee, Pierre really does know how to wake me up on a Saturday morning.*

"So, tonight, my friend Kaya is taking part in Wandsworth's Got Talent, and she needs all the support she can get. I told her I'd bring a plus one… and you're the plus one!"

"But tonight, I'm watching the Liverpool match with—"

"Seven p.m., Wandsworth Town Hall, don't be late! If you need a lift, let me know. Ooh and bring your new snazzy jacket too. *Namaste*, Mr Mills"

Before I can even say no, Izzy has already turned and marched out of my front garden, with the yoga mat stuffed under her arm. She's like a walking rainbow dressed from head-to-toe in colourful tie-dye yogi clothing. As her wild and frizzy curls bobble down the street,     I give out a call, "Izzy... Izzy!"

Great. This is all I need. Crazy yoga lady demands I shan't watch the football. Thankfully, she didn't ask any more questions about my performance at Percy's, but I still need to conjure up a plan. What should I do with my magic jacket?

I mean what would you do? Say you've found a potentially magic jacket; would you tell the whole town? Or would you lock it away and keep it a secret?

*The jacket literally has a mind of its own. Is it even safe to take outside? Can I even control it?*

*How will I decide?*

Well... I could flip a coin, or I could use that age-old technique of deciding for myself. I'll flip a coin! If anything the suspense will add a little spice to my Saturday morning. Heads means I have to bring Blue's jacket to the competition; tails means it stays at home.

I rummage through the pot of loose change at the front door, and pull out a shiny fifty pence piece that looks brand new.

OK, here we go, the big flick coming right up.

I punch the bottom of the coin, sending it high into the sky.

*Tinnnnng.*

*Woosh...*

*Woosh...*

*Woosh...*

The fifty pence piece is flying through the air, turning majestically as silver light glimmers from its surface.

*CLONK!*

*CLONK!*

*CLONK!*

It smashes against the wooden floor of our hallway,

It's spinning…spinning…and… it's stopped.

What is it?

It's landed on…

# Chapter 6

"Archie, so lovely to see you again with your snazzy new jacket. Why don't you put it on instead of carrying it under your arm?"

OK, you've guessed already, the coin landed on heads. I'm here at Wandsworth's Got Talent, but just to be safe, I've decided to carry Blue's Jacket instead.

"Kaya, this is Archie; Archie, this is Kaya," Izzy makes the introductions.

Kaya smiles while putting out her hand.

"Hey, Archie, thanks for coming and supporting me tonight."

Not only is Kaya really nice, she's super cool. Even her name is cool. You can tell she's going to be a style icon when she grows up. I can see it already; Kaya's name will be in lights, her face will be on billboards and on magazine covers too. She'll probably have her own fragrance called 'Perfume by Kaya'. Kaya is so cool, if she does one day have her own fragrance range, even I'd buy it.

"I wouldn't miss it for the world, Kaya. It's not like I had any other plans tonight. Isn't that right, Izzy?"

Izzy laughs before walking us up the steps of Wandsworth Town Hall. She turns and waves to her mum who waits in the car to make sure we get in safely.

Wandsworth Town Hall is absolutely beautiful. Lovely stained oak wood panelling adorns the walls, and the staircase looks like the one from the *Titanic*. It has that rich enchanting smell of a theatre that's entertained audience members for hundreds of years. We've got the venue, but have we got the talent? I better ask Kaya about tonight's competitors.

"Well, there's Alphabet Al, he can spell words backwards quicker than people can spell them forwards. He can also say the alphabet in reverse at the speed of light."

Is that even a talent? OK, I wonder who else is on the bill?

"Toilet Roll Tony" is the next name that Kaya rhymes off.

Toilet Roll Tony, is she making this up?

"A few years ago, Tony got really sick and couldn't leave the house, he was housebound for nearly six months. He absolutely loved football but couldn't leave the house to play, so instead, he learnt to do keepy ups with rolls of toilet paper. His mum said if you play football in the house, you'll break all my ornaments, so toilet roll was the next best thing. He's actually really good, he can do tricks, flicks, catch the roll behind his head and balance it on his nose."

"OK, this sounds like a crazy competition."

"It gets crazier; there was supposed to be a ninety-year-old breakdancing granny taking part but she had to pull out. Turns out, there's a spot going if you have any hidden talents."

Izzy butts in, "Archie is full of talents, you should've seen him in Percy's Rags yesterday, he was totes amazeballs."

I quickly intervene, "Enough talking, Izzy, let's grab our seats before the show starts. Good luck, Kaya, you'll hear us cheering from the front."

Kaya walks off and makes her way backstage to the artist area.

A voice from behind the red satin theatre curtain bellows, "Ladies and gentlemen, please welcome your host to the stage, Mr Dick Daniels!"

The crowd goes wild for Dick, Wandsworth's local funny man.

"It's a pleasure to be here tonight, and what a night it's going to be! We've got the best talent in all of Wandsworth, but unfortunately, they couldn't be here tonight, so this lot will have to do instead."

*Very funny, Dick*, the crowd is laughing their heads off already.

"Tonight's winner will be a thousand pounds richer by the end of this evening, and not only will they walk away with the coveted Wandsworth's Got Talent trophy, they'll also get to perform at the Mayor's Ball. So please go mad for your first act, Alphabet Andy."

Another voice shouts from behind the curtain.

"It's AL!"

Despite Dick's big ears, he didn't quite hear the message from behind the curtain.

"One more time, everybody, for Alphabet Andy."

An angry-looking man storms onto the stage.

"It's AL... AL! Two letters, it's not that hard to remember, is it?"

Alphabet Al looks annoyed but he gets on with the show.

"Oh, never mind... Give me a cheer if you like letters."

The crowd cheer,

*WAHEYY*

"Well, here's twenty-six for you.

"Z Y X W V U T S R Q P O N M L K J I H G F E D C B A."

*WOOSH*

Amazingly, Alphabet Al says the Alphabet backwards at the speed of light, the crowd gasps.

"What's your name, madame?"

AL is pointing towards a lady in the front row.

"Sheila," shouts the lady.

"OK, Sheila, how about a little bet? If I can spell your name backwards, quicker than you can spell it forwards, you owe me ten pounds! How does that sound?"

Without hesitation, Sheila shouts, "Deal."

"OK, we'll go on my count... Three, two, one. A L I E H S.

And that, my friends, is how you spell Sheila backwards."

Not only did Sheila lose the bet, she also spelt her own name wrong.

"The magnificent Alphabet Andy, everybody," Dick is back on stage and he makes the same mistake again.

"How many times do I have to tell you, it's AL!"

Al doesn't look happy.

"Thank you, Andy, well done. Now, ladies and gentlemen, please give it up for your next act, Toilet-Roll-Tonyyy!"

Tony takes to the stage kicking a toilet roll twenty feet into the air which he gracefully catches behind his neck. Tony then flicks the roll back up into the air. As it plummets towards the ground, he introduces another roll, now juggling both of them on his right foot.

Up into the air, both rolls go again as Tony starts to walk on his hands, while doing keepy-ups as both rolls bounce from the soles of his feet.

For his finale, Tony kicks both rolls so high into the air they crash off the stage lights on the ceiling. Astonishingly, Tony does a backflip and catches the rolls between his legs before they manage to hit the ground.

The crowd goes bananas shouting Tony's name. Tony was very good, but watching him playing with toilet roll has made me want to go to the bathroom.

"Talk about talent and we're only getting started. Now, our next act puts the 'K' in 'Kool'."

Dick clearly can't spell, and Alphabet Al angrily shouts from the side of the stage, "Cool is spelt with a 'C', not a 'K'!" Al's face is now as red as a tomato, he looks like he's about to explode.

"I want you to clap, whistle and scream for a lady who is going to be the next big pop superstar. Please give it up for our youngest competitor of the evening, it's Kayaaaa!"

Four men walk onto the stage; they must be Kaya's band. There's a drummer, a guitarist, a bass guitar player and a guy on the keyboard, and here comes Kaya.

She wheels onto the stage in a pair of rollerblades, zooming from one side to the other.

You have no idea how cool Kaya is. She's cooler than the North Pole. Cooler than a fridge freezer.

Kaya is so cool; she makes space seem boring.

She's dancing while singing, and singing while rollerblading. She's incredible! Her voice is angelic yet edgy, as she raps over the top of a funky beat, before singing the chorus one more time.

Kaya's song finishes and she blades past her band, slapping each of them with a zipping high five.

Dick comes back on stage.

"The wonderful Kaya, everybody."

Kaya takes a bow before whizzing off backstage. It's pretty obvious she's going to win tonight's competition, unless a freak accident takes place.

"Truly amazing. Now, folks, unfortunately, Greta, The Breakdancing Granny, can no longer compete in tonight's competition, so we have a slot that needs filled by one of you lot, our lovely audience. So who is brave enough to come up here and perform their special talent tonight?"

The crowd goes silent as Dick surveys the room looking for a volunteer.

"Any takers out there? Anyone at all?"

As a wave of eerie silence sweeps over Wandsworth Town Hall, Izzy's hand shoots into the air.

"Over here!"

Oh no! Big mouth is trying to set me up to perform.

"Could we get some lighting on this person, please?"

Dick instructs the lighting technician to swing the spotlight onto the crowd which now beams onto Izzy and I.

"Would you like to perform, young lady?" asks Dick.

Izzy elbows me in the ribs.

"No not me, but my friend Archie would love to get on stage."

"No, no, no, there's been a massive mistake, a colossal misunderstanding, I don't want to perform at all, thank you very much."

"Ladies and gentlemen, give the lad some support and encouragement!" demands Dick.

Before I can even run out the exit door, the crowd of five hundred people start chanting my name.

"Archie, Archie, Archie."

Even Izzy is cheering me on.

"Go on, Archie, you can do it, just do what you did in Percy's… Here, take this!"

Izzy holds up and passes over Blue's coat, it's been hanging on the back of my chair all night.

*Deary me, what mess have I gotten myself into! Ah well, what's the worst that can happen, right?*

I stand up from my seat and the crowd cheers even louder, I can barely hear my ears.

"Archie, Archie, Archie!"

Just as I see Kaya's band members leaving the stage I quickly slip on Blue's jacket.

It's happening again!

"Hey guys, help a brother out; how about staying on for one more song and giving me a beat?"

What did I just say? Those words would never have come out of my mouth, but every time I put on this coat I change into a completely different person. My body fizzes up like a bottle of cola as I walk down the aisle towards the stage.

It's like I can't even control my own body any more. My legs start to twitch and my hips begin to shake, I'm wiggling my bum and my feet are shuffling towards the microphone. It's about to happen again.

*"I said a one, two, a one, two, three, four..."*

*Uh oh, here comes the singing.*

*"Now here's a story about a boy named Blue*

*An ordinary kid like me and you,*

*He liked to have fun but he worked real hard,*

*He knew the harder he worked, would make him a star,*

*So every day he tried*

*And to his surprise,*

*It's true.*

*If you work, work, work a little harder,*

*You'll be fast, quick and a little sharper,*

*You'll be big, clever and a little smarter,*

*If you work, work, work a little harder,*

*Just give it your best,*

*And you'll start to feel blessed*

*It's true..."*

*HOLY MACKEREL!*

All of the five hundred people in the audience are now on their feet. They're clapping, filming and screaming my name. The lighting from their phones, illuminates Wandsworth Town Hall like fireflies in the night sky.

I look at Kaya's band members who are standing in shock, they can't believe it either.

Dick comes running towards me. "In all my years of showbiz, I have never witnessed a performance like that, what's your name, son?"

I'm panting after my performance but somehow manage to get a few words out. "Archie, Archie Mills…"

Dick looks me in the eye and says, "Son, you're going to be famous, you're going to be a star!

"The Amazing Archie Mills everybody, Amazing Archie the Singing Sensation!"

*YEYYYYYYY*
*WAHEYYYY*
*WOOHOOO*

# Chapter 7

Not only did I win the competition, I was on the front page of every newspaper in London the following morning. And how did I know that?

"Mr Mills, you're famous, you're on ze front page of *Ze Londoner*."

Pierre was holding the paper in front of my very eyes for all to see

Anytime my family gets good news, we come to Pierre's. It's a family tradition, it's how we like to celebrate. That time my dad got the promotion at Mountgammy Money Limited, we came here. When my mum came first in the parents' race at school sports day, we came here. We've always done that. And this time, it's on me, because this thirteen-year-old kid is now a thousand pounds richer.

"I've never had a celebrity in my cafe before, so today your family's food is on the house. Totally free! What would you like, my friends?"

This is crazy, I sing a silly little song and now I'm getting the VIP treatment at Pierre's. And I can't even spend the money I won.

"Better still, you guys take a seat and I'll bring you a selection of tasty pastries fresh from ze oven. Only ze best for ze Mills family."

I couldn't believe it,    I've never been in the paper before. Apart from that one time my mum sent in a photo for my tenth birthday, but this was different.

"Amazing Archie the Singing Sensation," Mum reads the headline of *The Londoner* and she's beaming from ear-to-ear. "My little star, we never knew you could sing," says Mum.

Nor did I...

I didn't even plan to go to the competition, let alone win it, and now I'm on the front page of *The Londoner*, getting free coffee and pastry... for my entire family.

Just as Pierre arrives at our table with tasty French treats stacked high on a cake stand, I'm surprised by yet another bombshell.

"Archieeeeee! I was just on my way to your house."

Izzy rushes through the door with a mountain of newspapers, plonking herself at our table.

"Morning, Mr and Mrs Mills, I'm not sure if you've heard the news but your son is pretty much famous. Check this out!"

Izzy holds up each paper reading the headlines one by one.

"*London Live: A Musical Masterclass.*"

"*London Times: Archie's Got Talent.*"

"*London Latest: The Boy in the Fur Coat.*"

"Everybody knows your name, mate, I've just come from Nando's Newsagents and your face is plastered over every shelf!"

Izzy is bouncing with excitement while stuffing her face with Pierre's freshly piped macarons.

None of this makes any sense, how has this happened?

I know... It's all happened because of Izzy. Had she not have taken me to Percy's Rags, we wouldn't be sitting here right now. I want to thank her, so I take a one hundred-pound note from my pocket and slip it across the table.

"What are you doing?" whispers Izzy.

"This is a token of my appreciation, a gift from me to you. You are my friend and none of this would've happened without you," I reply.

Izzy grabs the one hundred-pound note, holding it up to the light.

"WOAH! I've never seen a one hundred-pound note before; do you know how many yoga mats I could buy with this?"

Everybody at the table laughs, it's nice to see Izzy happy.

You know my mum always told me 'sharing is caring', so I slip another one hundred pound note across the table.

"Archie, what are you doing?"

Izzy is getting increasingly suspicious.

"Don't worry, this one's for Kaya. I figured Kaya deserved some of the money too. She would've won the competition had it not have been for the magic—"

I stop dead in my tracks, before blurting out the next word. Before I even get to finish my sentence, Izzy already has the second one hundred-pound note firmly in her grasp.

"This is so kind, Archie, Kaya is going to be so happy. You have a heart of gold. What are you going to do with the rest?" says Izzy.

I look at Mum and Dad with a rye smile, knowing they'll be impressed by what I'm about to say next.

"Well, my mum also told me to save a little for a rainy day. You never know when you might need an emergency cash stash. So even if it's raining cats and dogs, I'll still have eight hundred pounds in the bank; that's a hell of a lot of food from Borough Market."

*DING*

*DING*

*DING*

Izzy's phone vibrates so violently it nearly bounces off the table.

"Speaking of Kaya, she's just sent me a text. JEEPERS CREEPERS!"

Izzy jumps out of her chair and nearly falls to the floor.

"Archie, you're on the news!"

Izzy turns her phone round for everyone to see. I really am, I'm on the news!

"Meet the thirteen-year-old singing sensation. Archie Mills has become an overnight Internet hit after a clip of his performance at Wandsworth's Got Talent goes viral. The video has been watched more than five million times in the past twenty-four hours."

I can't believe it, the news presenter that we watch every day has just said my name.

Not only that, a clip of me singing has been watched more than five million times!

*MWAH*

Izzy jumps up, hugs me and kisses me on the cheek.

"My best friend is famous!"

If truth be told, I'm just a normal person with a normal life. I've never wanted to be famous, as Dad is about to remind me.

"Slow down, buster, let's not let the fame get to our heads. You don't want to count your chickens before they hatch. Remember, you're the son of an accountant..."

There's a saying "slow and steady wins the race". That saying sums up Dad; he's a tortoise, an accountant, a safe pair of hands. He doesn't make rash, off-the-cuff decisions, which I suppose is a good thing.

He's just trying to keep me grounded but it's hard to contain the excitement. Plus, I want to run home and make sure Blue's jacket is safe and sound.

"Mum, Dad, is it OK if I quickly run home to check on something?"

They give me their blessing.

"OK, but be safe, not too fast!" says Dad.

I quickly say my goodbyes, hugging Izzy and high-fiving Pierre as I leave with a belly full of pastry. I've eaten enough pastry to cover the whole of the Eiffel Tower.

Surely Izzy was exaggerating, I can't possibly be on the front page of every newspaper, can I?

Uh oh, I am…

I pop my head through the door of the corner shop and Nando the newsagent nearly jumps over the counter to check if it's me.

"Hey, wait a minute, you're that guy!"

*ZOOOOOOOM*

"Catch me if you can, Nando." I turn on my heels and sprint out of the shop, running down the street while laughing at how bonkers my morning has been.

It's all very exciting, but my life has completely flipped upside down in less than twenty-four hours.

It's not like you can practice 'how to become an overnight success', it just happens.

And when it does happen, life gets crazier by the second, as I'm about to find out…

The beautiful thing about Wandsworth Town is everything is 'just around the corner'. Izzy only lives a street away and Pierre's is merely two hundred yards from my front door and the station; I can see it from my bedroom window.

Just as I turn onto Oakhill Road, I see a middle-aged man parked right outside my house. He's dressed in a blue pinstripe suit and leaning on a green convertible sports car. It looks like he's waiting for me.

"Hey kid, the name's Andy, Andy from Astounding Artists."

Andy is small in stature but he has a big bulging belly, which is giving the buttons on his bright white shirt a run for their money. He chews gum vigorously.

"Listen, kid, I'm gonna cut to the chase. I saw the video clip of your performance last night, you blew my socks off!"

I guess that's a compliment, right?

"Who's your agent?" asks Andy.

"My agent? I don't have an agent." Unless he's talking about my mum and dad.

"You mean to say you ain't got one? Here…" Andy holds up his business card. "How do you fancy joining Astounding Artists? We've got everyone on our books, every type of entertainer you can think of. Singers, dancers, actors, actresses, stuntmen, stuntwomen, directors, models, heck we've even got clowns, quite a few actually. So, whatcha say, kid?"

I'm on the news, in the papers and now a strange man is offering me his business card right outside my house. What am I supposed to say? Right now, I wouldn't be surprised if a zebra cycled past me.

"I'd have to say… I'll have to ask my mum and dad first!"

Andy looks surprised by my mature and well-calculated response.

"OK, kid. Talk it over with your folks. They'd be mad not to let you sign with Astounding Artists. After all, who wouldn't want their son to be a star in Hollywood."

*HOLLYWOOD!*

How is it even possible to go from Wandsworth Town to Hollywood in less than twenty-four hours?

"Sleep on it, kid, let me know first thing on Monday morning."

Andy hops back into his car, buckles his seatbelt and slides on his sunglasses.

*\*Vrrrooommm\**

*\*Vrrrooommm\**

*\*Screechhhhh\**

Andy's tyres squeal across the tarmac and he speeds off into the sunset, leaving me standing outside my house confused, and asking lots of questions. Like, what just happened? How did he know where I lived? And why do I smell like burnt rubber?

# Chapter 8

***BING***
> ***BING***
> ***BING***
> ***BING***

It's Monday morning and my alarm clock is rattling around my bedside table like a bucking bronco.

Mondays usually start with a moan and a groan but this Monday is extra special, because it's the first of the summer holidays and another adventure looms.

Mum and Dad couldn't believe Andy popped by our house yesterday. And it seems like good news spreads fast, because Mr Mountgammy has invited me to his office for lunch. Dad says Mr Mountgammy saw me on the news and he wants to celebrate by throwing a party.

But the big news today is, for the first time in my entire life, I'll be riding the train solo.

Look at me go, Archie Mills the grown up riding the 'Grown-up Express' all by himself. *Choo choo!*

After a quick change, I'm ready to leave, but before I do I have to say goodbye to Blue's jacket.

"Byeeeee, miss you already!"

Did I actually just say goodbye to a coat? I think I'm losing my marbles.

What a glorious day! The skies are blue and the birds are tweeting. I even have time to grab a porridge pot from the Railway Coffee kiosk.

And here it comes, the 11 a.m. Wandsworth to Waterloo train.

"All aboard now," shouts the platform manager as the doors fly open. A carriage full of empty seats awaits.

Maybe Mondays aren't so bad after all, I'll not have to stand. I take a seat and tuck into my hearty breakfast.

*FLASH*

"I hope you don't mind, it's for my daughter, she's watched your video ten times already."

*WOW, LADY!* Here I am stuffing my face, and a complete stranger blinds me with her camera.

"Do you think we could get a selfie together? Melissa is such a big fan," says the lady sitting opposite me.

*A fan! OK, this is weird! I now have a fan!*

"Say cheeeeese."

*FLASH*

It doesn't look like I have a choice; as porridge dangles from my lip, a lady who I've just met fifteen seconds ago has her arm slung around my shoulder, snapping selfies.

"Ooh, what a lovely picture, I'll have to get it framed and hung on the living room wall. Melissa will love it. Thanks, Archie."

Crazy selfie lady even knows my name!

"This is my stop, pleasure bumping into you Archie."

Crazy selfie lady waves at me before getting off.

If I thought that was weird, my Monday was about to get even weirder.

I hop off at the next stop and walk towards Dad's office.

As I pass through the revolving doors of Mountgammy Money Limited, everybody in the lobby stops what they're doing.

People are staring at me like I've arrived riding a fire-breathing dragon. But they're smiling and waving just like crazy selfie lady did , even Grumpy Graham the security guard said hello. Dad says Graham never says hello to anyone; *Why am I so special?*

I make it over to the glass elevator.

*DING*

"Archie, my little accountant in the making, you made it here all by yourself."

Dad proudly stands in the middle of the elevator. He pulls me in and ruffles my hair before crouching down to my level.

"Bud, you're the talk of the town around here. Everybody wants to meet you."

*Oh gosh!*

The elevator rockets upwards, eventually stopping at the top floor. The doors slide open and just as we walk around the corner, we're greeted by a wall of applause.

A hundred men and women from my dad's office are clapping, whopping, whistling and hollering.

There's balloons, banners and confetti everywhere.

"Here he is, ladies and gentlemen, the man of the moment, the singing sensation, Mr Archie Mills."

Mr Mountgammy stands with his arms aloft, encouraging more cheering.

"Archie, Archie, Archie!"

Grown men four times my age are celebrating like they've just won the World Cup.

"Son, I've never been prouder in all my life, watching you on the news was like watching my own child ride a bike for the very first time. And when you make me proud, you make my company proud, and when that happens, there's only one thing left     to do, and that's celebrate. Julie, bring in the cake."

Julie is the second highest employee at Mountgammy Money Limited, she is my dad's boss' boss and now she's bringing me cake!

And what a cake it is; seven tiers' tall with sparklers on each tier, cream and jam oozing out the sides of each layer. It's the size of a Christmas tree and multicoloured like a rainbow. Red, orange, yellow, green, blue, purple and pink, and at the very top there's a miniature statue of me holding a microphone made from icing sugar.

"What do you think, son?" smiles Mr Mountgammy.

"It's... glorious, just glorious!" I don't really know what else to say, but wonder in awe.

"Grab yourself a slice and come to my office for a chat when you're done. Bring your dad too."

*HUH! Mr Mountgammy is inviting me into his office?*

"Dig in, folks," shouts Mr Mountgammy before walking down the corridor.

Right now, Dad is so excited, his eyeballs look as if they're about to pop out of his head.

"Archie, in my twenty years of working here, I've never been invited into Mr Mountgammy's office. You only get invited if you're a VIP. That means, you're a very important person."

As Dad grits his teeth in a fevered frenzy, his colleagues form a circle around the cake cart. I smile awkwardly towards the sea of blue and grey suits.

Julie pulls out a shiny cake knife and starts cutting from the top.

*\*PLONK\**

"Here you go, Archie, you deserve the biggest slice."

Julie hands me a piece of cake the size of my head, and boy does it look good. Talking about heads, I think that's the first part I'll eat, the head of my very own icing sugar statue.

*NOM*

*NOM*

*NOM*

*Mmm, this sure is a delicious cake, who knew my head would taste so good.*

"C'mon, let's go see Mountgammy," says Dad.

# Chapter 9

***KNOCK***

    ***KNOCK***

"Come in, son."

Mr Mountgammy's office is just what I expected it to be. It smells like... success.

It smells like power, money and expensive leather.

On the wall is a photo of Mr Mountgammy, and beside that is a photo of Mr Mountgammy Senior, and next to that is a portrait of Great Mr Mountgammy and then at the very end there's an even bigger portrait of Great-Great Mr Mountgammy.

"Take a seat, son. Same to you, Mr Mills. Make yourselves at home."

*What does Mountgammy want? Why am I in his office?*

"Son, if there's one thing I like in life, it's talent. We've all got it, but some of us choose to use it more than others. The only thing that beats talent is hard work. You could be the most talented man in the world, but if you don't work hard, you may as well have no talent at all."

*Where is Mr Mountgammy going with this speech?*
I wonder.

"Clearly, you're both talented and hardworking, and a little birdie tells me you're quite the whizz with numbers. So, how would you like to be a Junior Apprentice Accountant right here at Mountgammy Money Limited, with a summer job and a desk right next to your dad? Better still, how would you like me to promote your father, Mr Mills, to Executive Accounts Manager? That'd be his second successive company promotion..."

Dad jumped in without hesitation, "We'll take it."

*CRIKEY!* Hold your horses, Dad. I mean sure, this is an offer I can't refuse, but a minute's thought wouldn't hurt nobody.

"And maybe one day, if you work hard enough, you could have your very own photo on that wall next to four generations of Mountgammy's. You could be the son I never had... What do you say... son?"

Dad looks like he's about to cry. He wants this so bad.

Now I didn't plan the next part at all, but "Can I use the bathroom?" is the first thing to come out of my mouth.

"I wasn't quite expecting you to say that," replied Mr Mountgammy, "but take your time, son, we'll be waiting right here."

I make a little joke on my way out the door, "It must be the cake, I guess that's what happens when you eat your own head."

Dad's laugh is so over the top and dramatic, he could win an Oscar for 'best actor'.

"Funny and clever; he sure is a catch, Mr Mountgammy."

I nervously dash to the toilet.

Mr Mountgammy is making me an offer I can't refuse, and Dad is clinging onto his every last word, but I need a few minutes to think about this in private.

For some reason, I've decided that the best place to do this thinking is in a smelly toilet cubicle at my dad's office, and boy did it smell.

*Eughhhhh*! This toilet is a total stinkfest!

I close the cubicle door behind me, pull down the seat to sit on and just as I do,

**Buzzzzzzzzzzz***

***Buzzzzzzzzzzz***

***Buzzzzzzzzzzz***

My phone is vibrating and shaking in my pocket. Who could this possibly be?

"Morning, kid. Andy here from Astounding Artists?"

Jiminy Cricket, how did Andy get my number? And why is he ringing me right this very second?

What Andy doesn't know is I'm about to make the biggest decision of my entire life.

Talk about perfect timing...

"Listen, kid, I'm with your sweet mum, Pauline. I've been telling her about us fine folk at Astounding Artists and how we think we can make you a star!"

Well, this really is quite the quandary. Dad is with Mountgammy, Mum is with Andy and I'm currently in a smelly toilet cubicle.

"Hello, Archie, my love, it's Mum here, you're on loudspeaker. Andy called by the house today, and I think you really ought to come meet him and have a proper chat. This really is a once-in-a-lifetime opportunity, dear."

There's an old saying about being 'stuck between a rock and a hard place', which means you're in a very tricky position, and I most certainly am in a right pickle.

What is the correct decision to make?

Do I play it safe, stay here and stick with Dad and Mr Mountgammy, or do I take a once-in-a-lifetime opportunity that I might regret not taking?

It looks like I'm just going to have to tell Andy and Mum about my dilemma.

"You see, Andy, I'm stuck between a rock and a hard place... Mr Mountgammy has just offered me a summer job as a Junior Apprentice Accountant, and he's offered Dad a promotion too. Which means more money for the family, Mum."

This really is an awful predicament to find oneself in.

"You can be an accountant all your life, kid, you only get one shot at Hollywood, and Hollywood doesn't wait for anybody."

*GREAT!*

Another spanner in the works. My decision can't get any harder, the size of the decision facing me is about as big as Mount Everest, and that's big.

My head says 'Mountgammy'.

But my heart says 'Hollywood'.

And my gut says 'I've eaten too much cake'.

There's only one way I can possibly decide...

"Kid, you still there?"

Andy is shouting down the other end of the phone thinking I've vanished.

The shiny fifty pence piece that I used to make my decision on the day of Wandsworth's Got Talent is still in my pocket. I guess it's been a good luck charm ever since. I pull it out of my pocket.

*TING*

*WOOSH*

*WOOOSH*

*WOOOOSH*

I've flipped this coin for the second time in as many days, again it spins high into the sky, nearly flying over the top of the cubicle door. I'll call it in the air...

Heads, I stay here!

Tails, I go to Hollywood!

*WOOSH*

*WOOOSH*
*THWACK*

My shiny silver coin crashes back down to earth, landing flat on the floor.

What's it landed on?

What is it?

It's…

# Chapter 10

"Hop in, kid," smiles Andy.

Thirty minutes ago, I was sitting in a smelly toilet cubicle flipping a coin that would decide my future, now I'm sitting in Andy's green convertible next to Mum.

In less than half an hour, I've:

*Declined Mr Mountgammy's generous offer of a job

*Told Dad that I'm leaving for Hollywood

*And I've also walked away from a seven-tier cake

I've never seen Dad look so sad. He waved us off from outside his office, then trudged back into work, deflated, dejected, with his shoulders slumped.

As the wind flies through my hair, I think to myself, *Could this be the silliest decision of my life?*

I hope not...

I feel like I've aged ten years in the last thirty minutes, surely this isn't the average day of a thirteen-year-old boy?

"OK, so we've got a busy day ahead of us, kid! Here's how the schedule is looking:

Twelve p.m. — Sign the contract at Astounding Artists

One p.m. — Meet your new stylist, Fabio

Two p.m. — Lunch

Three p.m. — Photoshoot with *Star Weekly*

Four p.m. — Autographs and photographs with fans

Five p.m. — Dinner

Six p.m. — TV interview on *London Live News*

Seven p.m. — Drive home and pack for La La Land.

And then you can go to sleep and dream big, because tomorrow morning, we're going to Hollywood, baby."

*HOLLYWOOD?*

*TOMORROW MORNING?*

*ARE YOU FOR REAL?*

"That's right, kid, there's no business, like show business?"

Andy smiles in his rear-view mirror, as Mum pinches me with excitement.

Before we know it, we're walking down the corridor of Astounding Artists, passing framed photos of all the famous stars who've worked here in the past. Living legends, Hollywood Royalty.

Mum can hardly contain herself.

"Look, there's Tommy the Muscle Man who wrestled the wild tiger in the movie *Tommy and The Tiger*. And Chi Chi Mazooku, the actress and ballet dancer who married the president of the United States of America."

We arrive at the next framed photo outside Andy's office, but it's blank. Maybe they're saving a space for Amazing Archie the Singing Sensation.

Andy's office is so cool. There's a glass bowl full of chocolate sweets sitting in the middle of his glass table, a row of mini fridges with every type of fizzy drink imaginable and a popcorn machine next to a wall full of plaques, trophies and awards.

This is the second time in half a day that I've been in a swanky office with one of my parents.

"Here you are, kid, the piece of paper that's going to change your life forever."

### 'CONTRACT OF EMPLOYMENT
### 'ASTOUNDING ARTISTS'

Andy slides the contract across the table, crisp white sheets of paper dazzle in front of my eyes. The words 'CONTRACT OF EMPLOYMENT' stand out, like skyscrapers.

"Have a read, kid, sign it and, before you know it, your face    will be on my wall, and on every child's bedroom wall across the country. Better still, you'll be on every magazine, billboard and TV screen around the world."

Andy sits back in his chair, plonking his feet on his desk and planting his hands behind his head.

This does sound pretty life-changing.

"And remember, kid, if you can see it in your mind, you can hold it in your hand!"

"Anything is possible. You just gotta dream it, breathe it and believe it."

**DREAM IT**
**BREATHE IT**
**BELIEVE IT**

Andy's right, anything is possible!

I could've had my photo on the wall of Mountgammy Money Limited, but instead I'm choosing to have it on a billboard in the USA.

"Archie, remember when you were younger, we used to practice your autograph? Remember I used to say 'you need to practice your autograph in case someone asks for it?' Well, today is that day, Archie?"

Mum holds up the pen, gesturing for me to take it. Her eyes are shining like diamonds. She wants this as bad as Dad wanted his promotion.

"Remember my tip for the perfect autograph, Archie... Make sure you have enough loops and squiggles in it so your name pops off the page. That's how people will remember you!"

It's time to sign, time to shine.

Here goes nothing.

And how about a smiley face to finish with, because a happy face makes people happy.

Mum hugs me and kisses me on the side of the cheek.

"OK, kid, let's get you down the stairs to Fabio, he's the best stylist in all of Italy. Prepare to be blown away."

Andy pounces to his feet and leads us out of his office.

# Chapter 11

I've never had a stylist before, except for my mum of course; she's been dressing me since I was little. I guess this means she can now retire and put her feet up.

Andy leads us down a spiral staircase below his office. The deeper down the steps we go, the louder the pop music in the background becomes. It sounds like someone's having a disco down here.

We pass through a beaded curtain door to be met by a fanfare of exuberance.

"*Ciao*, Mr Archie, come in, come in…"

This must be the fabulous Fabio!

"And who is this young lady beside you? Your sister?"

Mum starts to blush; we've only been in the room ten seconds and Fabio is already dishing out the compliments.

"No, I'm his mum, and I'm old enough to be your mum too." Mum smirks.

You can tell Fabio is a pro, this isn't his first rodeo.

"OK! So, my job is to make you look *freddo*! Do you know what *freddo* means, Archie?"

I really can't say that I do, Fabio will have to explain.

"It means cool in Italian; we need to make you look cool."

With his flowing long blonde hair and glowing Italian tan, Fabio swans around his underground clothing emporium with pizazz. He dances us past rails upon rails of outfits; sparkles, sequins, feathers and fur, that stretch as far as the eye can see.

"First, we need to get rid of this boring looking suit, it doesn't do anything for you, my love."

Thanks, Fabio… That's very kind of you to say.

"We need to bring out your personality, and we can't do that dressed like this. You can be whatever you want, whoever you want, all with the change of an outfit! You can be an astronaut, a pilot, hell you can be Count Dracula if you really wish! Fashion is life, darling! And this outfit is death."

Fabio really is full of compliments today.

"So let's start by saying goodbye to your current clothes and give them a new home. In the corner, you'll see a recycling bin, pop them in there, please. You see, I tell all my clients they have to

**RECYCLE!**

**RECYCLE!**

**RECYCLE!**

"You don't have to buy new clothes all the time, that trend is so overrated and outdated. Go second-hand shopping, I do it all the time. Vintage, pre-owned, pre-loved clothes are the best! Do you know what thrift shopping is, Archie?"

Of course, I know full well what thrift shopping is; if it weren't for Izzy's trip to Percy's Rags, I'd be sitting at home twiddling my thumbs waiting for a football match to start

"We need to use our imagination. You see, that recycling bin is full of treasure; pure gold. With a little TLC, a sewing machine and a new button or two, your old clothes could be the next must-have outfit at a Milan fashion show. We need to look after our planet, we don't need to

*MAKE*

*MAKE*

*MAKE*

What do I say we need to do instead,

*RECYCLE*

*RECYCLE*

*RECYCLE*

OK, enough of my Oscar-winning speech, HEADS UP!"

*WOOSH*

*WOOSH*

*WOSSSHH*

Fabio throws half a dozen jackets into the air and they're flying towards me like birds falling from the sky.

"Good catch, Mr Archie! Now, I don't like secrets, and I can't keep secrets. Some would say I'm loose lipped, so I must tell you. In two days' time, you're going to be singing on *The Ella Show*, the most watched TV chat show in all of America. So you're going to need a staple piece of clothing that people will remember you by. A jacket, a special trademark jacket that catches the eye."

Fabio claps his hands with enthusiasm.

"But I already have a…"

Before I even get to finish my sentence, Fabio pushes me through a curtain and into a dressing room where a collection of jeans, trousers, hats, shoes and t-shirts await.

By the sounds of things, I'm not the only person that Fabio's clothes and accessories awaits.

"Mrs Mills, we can't have you missing out on all the fun. Why don't you help yourself to the handbag shelf down the back while Archie tries on his clothes? Treat yourself to one or two items, courtesy of Italy's most splendid stylist… me, of course."

I can't see through this curtain, but I can already tell that Mum will be smiling; she loves handbags.

How crazy has my life just become!

*The Ella Show!* I'm going to be appearing on *The Ella Show* with *The Queen of American TV*!

***GULP***

It's like I got on a rollercoaster at a theme park which keeps going faster and faster. There's no slowing down. A couple of days ago, no one knew my name, and now the biggest star on American TV is inviting me onto her show.

"How are we looking, Archie?"

I try on the first outfit and *nothing* happens.

The moment I tried on Blue's jacket in Percy's, a magical feeling swept over my body. Molecules, atoms and energy fizzed around from my head to my toe. I felt electric!

So far, I've tried on a black leather biker jacket with leather bottoms, a double-denim number, a space aged futuristic silver tracksuit and nothing. But there's more…

Facing me is a two-piece suit with dozens of American inspired badges stitched onto the body; the stars and stripes flag, the Statue of Liberty and dozens of hundred-dollar bills, just some of the iconic images spread across the suit's surface.

"Have you found the one yet, Archie, do you feel like a million bucks?"

I walk out to tell Fabio the truth, that I already have a coat, a magical coat, a coat that gives me a voice, a coat that belonged to a 1960s superstar, but as soon as I step out from the curtain, Fabio begins to cry like a cat.

"*Uhhhhhhhhhhhhhh! Belissimoooooooo! Freddo, freddo, freddo!* Never in my life have I seen something so beautiful, so breath-taking, so AMERICAN! This is the American Dream, Archie, and this is what you will wear on *The Ella Show*!"

"But, Fabio, I already have a..."

"You ready, kid, we're running behind, your shoot with *Star Weekly* starts in fifteen minutes. Let's walk and talk. Fabio, bring a rail of clothes."

Before I get to say anything, Andy halts the styling session, whisking us out of the underground clothing bunker and through a maze of corridors that run under Astounding Artists HQ.

"Wait for me!" shouts Mum, as she runs towards us with several handbags hooked around her arms.

I guess I'll just have to wait before I can tell Andy and Fabio about Blue's jacket.

# Chapter 12

"Work it, baby, work it… The camera loves you, Archie."

"OK, give me happy!"

"Beautiful. Now give me sad!"

"Yes… That's what I'm talking about! Excited, give me your excited face, Archie."

"These are great, really great. Now pout for me, Archie, pout and pretend you're a fish!"

*FLASH*

Phoebe the photographer sets her camera down.

"OK, guys, I think we've got the shot. THAT'S A WRAP! Beautiful work, team."

I thought Kaya was cool, but Phoebe the Photographer is next-level cool. She's dressed in denim dungarees, funky sports shoes and wearing a red neck scarf. Her laugh is hypnotic and she has the warmth of a hot radiator. Phoebe has the whole room eating from the palm of her hand. She's been directing us like puppets on strings, but she's super nice and really lovely. And here she comes.

*BOOM*

Phoebe fist pumps me and then fist pumps my mum.

"Archie, that was iconic."

"This could be the most iconic magazine cover of the new millennium."

"In fact, I will eat my hat if this isn't the all-time-greatest-selling edition of *Star Weekly*. You should be very proud, Mrs Mills."

Mum can hardly control her emotions, as she claps while bouncing up and down.

Phoebe smiles before walking back to her team to flick through the images on her laptop.

"Listen up, everybody, we need to keep our starman fed and hydrated; we've a busy day ahead. Bring in the catering cart," shouts Andy.

Out of nowhere, a snack table on wheels is hurried onto the studio floor. A mountain of breakfast bars, crisps, muffins, croissants and bottles of fizzy water make up the spread.

"Take five, Archie, and then we'll bring in your fans," says Andy.

I forgot I had fans... A magic jacket and a viral video later and now people want to meet me.

Usually, it's just the three amigos; Mum, Dad and I, and Izzy, of course, but now I'm Mr Popular.

"Let me teach you a thing or two about fans, kid! Fans are the lifeblood of what we do. Keep your fans happy and you'll be in showbusiness for years to come."

A few hours in and Andy is already showing me the ropes.

He has a table and chair combo set up in the corner of the studio, my very own meet and greet area, I better get comfy!

As I take my seat, Phoebe walks towards me holding a bunch of flyers.

"Pretty cool, huh, Archie?"

Wait a minute, we've just taken these pictures. Phoebe doesn't hang about. She's photographed me and printed out my flyer already! On the front of the flyer it says 'Amazing Archie the Singing Sensation' above a photo of my face. They look incredible.

"Merch… Original merchandise. Give them what they want, kid."

Andy winks before handing me a pen. He shouts to his assistant, "Bring in the fans."

*Oh boy, this is it! Here they come…*

"Remember what I said earlier Archie, make sure your autograph has lots of loops and squiggles, someday these flyers will be worth money," whispers Mum in my ear.

The first fan approaches. "Hi, Archie, I'm Melissa McCarthy from Archie's Army Fan Club."

*ARCHIE'S ARMY! I have a fan club?*

Melissa must only be seven years old and just a few feet tall, but she's marched in with the brazen confidence of an army general.

"I've even set up the Archie's Army webpage, which I coded all by myself."

A wise head on young shoulders, Melissa certainly knows her apples from her oranges.

"Ooh and before I forget, this, is for you."

Melissa hands me a black and white 'Archie's Army' badge, before patting hers with pride.

"You only get into Archie's Army if you're wearing one, it's the official seal of approval."

"Thanks, Melissa, that's very kind," I say.

"And this is my mother Dorothy... Dorothy McCarthy."

HOLD THE PHONE! I know her. It's crazy train lady! Crazy train lady is Melissa's mum?

"You guys have already met, on the 11 a.m. Wandsworth to Waterloo train, remember?"

How could I forget? Melissa pulls out a framed photo of Dorothy and I on the train. Yep, and there's the little piece of porridge dangling from my lip, how lovely!

"Do you think you could sign it, and after that do you think we could get a photo together?"

Melissa is smiling with her neck tilted and face scrunched up like a cute little pug. She's wearing braces and I can see all her teeth smiling back at me. And there's her puppy dog eyes too, which dazzle through her thick-rimmed glasses.

"How could I say no to the world's best fan!"

I throw my arm around Melissa's shoulder, just like her mum did on the train.

"Say cheese, guys." Dorothy is ready with her camera once again. "Three, two, one…"

**\*FLASH\***

"OK, let's keep this queue moving and get this show on the road." Andy claps his hands and brings forward the next fan.

"So wonderful to meet you once again, Archie. This means the world to Melissa. She knows everything about you; your date of birth, your middle name, where you bought your jacket from…"

MY JACKET? I hope that's all she knows about my jacket!

"I know everything, Archie. See you soon."

Melissa smiles and skips off, while giggling and waving back as she leaves the studio.

# Chapter 13

Day one of being a star and I've been styled, photographed, fed and greeted by fans, and it's not over yet.

We're back in Andy's green convertible on the way to the *Live in London* TV studios.

"When you're with Astounding Artists, it's 24/7 round the clock entertainment, 365 days a year."

How does Andy do it? Does he even sleep? He's three times my age and twice my size and he's bouncing around like the Easter bunny.

Mum is semi-snoozing in the back seat, I think she's had too much excitement for one day.

"I need a coffee," she grumbles.

***SCREEEEEECH***

Andy pulls off the main road, skidding through a roundabout towards a building covered in satellite dishes.

Mum slides from one end of Andy's leather seat to the other, crashing against the side of his car.

"Well, that's one way to wake up!" winces Mum as she straightens up.

It looks like we're here.

Andy slowly drives up the tree-lined entrance, there's a gorgeous green lawn being fed by water sprinklers, and a gardener pruning a hedge row in the shape of the *Live in London* logo. A huge TV screen is positioned in the middle of the lawn, showing rolling news stories from across the city.

"Every night without fail, your father watches *Live in London*, and tonight he'll be watching you, my love," says Mum while gazing at the giant TV screen.

Dad won't be the only person watching, he'll be joined by nine million others. OH BOY!

As we pull up to the front door, we're welcomed by a stylish, well-dressed man, full of bravado.

"Ahh, the Amazing Archie Mills, my name's Peter the Floor Manager. It's an absolute pleasure to meet you. Usually, my assistant collects our guests, but I wanted to see you in the flesh myself."

Peter is a friendly, jolly floor manager with a spring in his step. His job is to make sure the news programme runs smoothly. He's got fluffy black hair and a clipboard full of paper containing lots of important information. Nestling on top of his fluffy hair is a headset.

"That's Davy the Director shouting in my ear. He's the boss. Let me turn him down a little…"

Peter fiddles with his nob, lowering the volume of his headset.

"There we are, that's better. Let's take you straight through to makeup, not that you'll need much, a dashing young lad like yourself."

We hurry through a side door into makeup.

"Maria, let me introduce you to Amazing Archie the Singing Sensation," proclaims Peter.

Maria's makeup sanctuary has mirrored walls and strips of light bulbs that illuminate the room. A beautiful lavender powder smell fills the air.

"Archie! Come in, take a seat... Now, you just sit back and relax. I'm going to give you a light dusting of makeup that'll give you a golden TV glow."

Maria has a warm smile and pots upon pots of brushes and makeup utensils.

She slings a black cape around my shoulders.

I've never worn makeup before, except for that one time, Izzy dressed me up.

"Everybody wears makeup these days, Archie. Peter won't come to work without a little sunshine on his face."

Peter smiles in the reflection of the mirror, nodding in agreement.

"It's true, Archie, makeup is like a lick of paint on a rusty old fence, it brings you back to life."

WOW! It really does; my cheekbones have never looked so...good. They're like giant cliffs standing on the edge of my face. And my forehead, it's as smooth as a bowling ball.

Maria finishes up before handing me back to Peter.

"OK, Archie, I'm going to take you onto the studio floor. It's nearly time for your big TV debut!"

Mum and Andy give me a double thumbs up as I leave them for the very first time.

Peter walks me out of makeup past a flashing 'ON-AIR' sign that dazzles in bold red lettering.

My palms are clammy and my heart is pounding. I can't tell if I'm nervous or excited, or both.

We stop in front of a solid wooden door, a door that separates dreams from reality. This door is the only thing between me and every TV set in all of London.

As he quietly opens the door, Peter turns round and whispers back, "Take a deep breath, smile and remember to have fun."

Here goes nothing, my five minutes of fame coming right up.

"OK, guys, we're on a short ad break, let's get Archie into position."

This is it, Peter walks me over to the news desk, sitting me down opposite Donna T.

Donna smiles while ruffling her stack of paper.

"And we're back on air in five... four... three... two... one..."

Peter gives the signal, we're back on air.

"Hello and welcome back to *Live in London* with me, Donna T."

*Oh lordy, I'm on TV!*

Three giant cameras are pointing right in my face.

*Act cool, Archie, all you have to do is act cool!*

"Our next guest has become somewhat of an overnight Internet sensation, after a clip of the talented Archie Mills goes viral. This video of his winning performance at Wandsworth's Got Talent has been viewed more than ten million times in two days, and I'm delighted to be joined by the man himself. A very warm welcome to you, Archie."

Yep, right now, I'm smiling back at the entire city of London.

"So tell me, what does it feel like to be an Internet singing sensation?" asks Donna.

"Kinda cool, I get to come and hang out with nice people like you," I quickly reply.

"And what an amazing performance it was, how long have you been singing for, Archie?"

She's not going to believe me when I say this...

"Since Friday," I coolly respond.

"Since Friday! Anyone who learns to sing like that in a few days must have some kind of superpower?" shrieks Donna.

*Whatever you do, DON'T mention the magic jacket, laugh it off, Archie!*

"Hahaha... Well, I just opened my mouth and the words came flying out."

Donna looks bamboozled.

"What an incredible revelation. Can you believe it? The thirteen-year-old boy who never knew he could sing. Let's take another look at Archie in action, here's a clip of that winning performance at Wandsworth's Got Talent."

*Now here's a story about a boy named blue*
*An ordinary kid like me and you,*
*He liked to have fun but he worked real hard,*
*He knew the harder he worked, would make him a star.* *

Donna T is enjoying my performance, she's tapping her pen on the news desk and bobbing her head from side to side.

"Well, you can certainly sing, and you can certainly dance, maybe you'll treat the *Live in London* viewers to a special performance right now?"

UH OH!

HOUSTON, WE HAVE A PROBLEM!

Donna T is asking me to sing live on TV — without Blue's jacket!

*Say something, Archie, anything!*

…

…

…

…

What feels like the longest pause in the history of mankind is broken.

"Well… any chance of a song from the singing sensation that is Archie Mills?" Donna prods again.

I need to buy myself some time to think of an excuse.

"Er, I'd love to, but I can't!" is about all I can muster up.

"You can't… why?" Donna looks at me suspiciously, perplexed by my answer. After all, she is a journalist trained to ask inquisitive questions.

"Because, I'm…"

*Think, Archie, think! Any excuse, anything at all, you can't sing without Blue's jacket.*

"I can't because I'm… I'm… flying to America tomorrow. Yeah, that's right, I'm flying to America to perform on *The Ella Show*, so I need to save my voice!"

*HALLELUJAH! You're a genius, Archie, good answer.*

"OK, maybe you'll come back and give us a song another time. Well, that's all for tonight, folks, I'll be back at six p.m. tomorrow evening with all the latest news. Good night."

Donna closes the show and the red 'On-Air' lights around the studio suddenly fade to black.

Peter signals that we're off-air and we can now relax.

Andy rushes towards me, having made his way from make-up onto the studio floor. His smile is the shape of a coat hanger, he must be happy.

83

"Way t'a go, kid, you're a natural, it's like you've been doing this TV malarkey for years. And I like what you did back there, you didn't sing. If they want you to sing live on air, they better speak to your agent first, and hand over a big fat cheque. I'm proud of you, kid. Let's get you home."

HOME SWEET HOME!

Never have I been happier to hear those words.

Just as we're about to walk out the door, Donna T stops us dead in our tracks.

"Excuse me, Archie!"

What's she going to say?

"I shouldn't really ask but… Do you mind if we get a selfie together?"

I laugh to myself and think, *So this really is what it's like to be famous.*

"It'd be my pleasure…" I say.

# Chapter 14

*'Bonjour, Monsieur Archie, we watched you on Live In London, you were fantastique. Free pastries for life my friend. Au revoir, Pierre'*

*'Saw you on the news, everybody at Mountgammy Money is super proud, son. Ps I got your number from your dad. Regards, Mr Mountgammy'*

*'My best friend is on TV. Ahhhhhhhh. See you later, love Izzy xxx'*

My phone is ringing like a church bell; all my friends are sending me well wishes after my appearance on the news.

It's dinged and donged the whole way from the TV studios to Wandsworth Town.

Andy's car pulls onto Oakhill Road. At long last, we're back; what a day we've had.

Mum and I hop out as Andy leans over the edge of his convertible. "Heathrow Airport, nine a.m., Terminal two. Your mum and dad are going to bring you. Tomorrow is the first day of the rest of your life, Archie. See you in the morning, kid."

Andy winks before speeding off into the sunset.

"Ooh I can't wait to tell Dad about the adventure that we've had today," announces Mum with glee.

She skips through the front gate and up the path towards the front door.

"Honeyyy, we're home," shouts Mum, entering excitedly.

Mum dances into the kitchen to find Dad slouched over the table eating a bowl of cereal, his face is melancholic and his tie is loosened at the neck.

"Ooh, we really have had the most magnificent day dear Archie's a star, a star I tell you."

Dad doesn't respond as Mum rambles on while pottering around the kitchen.

"First, he signed a contract with Astounding Artists. Then we met his stylist, Fabio, an Italian, and what a lovely lad he was. He even gave me two handbags, for free! Look, aren't they beautiful darling!"

Unfazed, Dad's head remains hung over his cereal bowl, as he slurps milk from his spoon.

"After that, it was photographs for *Star Weekly* magazine, autographs with his fans and then the evening news. Did you see him on the news, dear; he was wonderful, just wonderful."

There's a sombre atmosphere in the kitchen, and it's wafting from Dad's side of the room. He hasn't said a peep or moved an inch.

"And tomorrow, our little man is flying to America to perform on *The Ella Show* in New York City."

Dad pounces to his feet, now engulfed with energy.

"AMERICA? With who?" gasps Dad.

Well, it certainly looks like someone has shaken the tiger's cage; Dad is now awake.

"With Andy from Astounding Artists, and Fabio too. You'll meet them in the morning, darling. They're sweethearts, they really are, dear."

Dad is pacing up and down the kitchen floor.

"You mean to say we're going to let our son fly to America with two strangers who we've known for ten minutes?"

I was hoping Dad would've been happy for me, but he seems annoyed. I've never seen him like this before.

*BUZZZZZZZZZZZZZZ*

Saved by the bell, it's the front door and it's perfect timing for me to escape.

"I'll get it," I chirp before dashing out of the kitchen, closing the door tightly behind me.

I can see Izzy's wild, untamed, frizzy hair through the front window pane, and boy am I glad she's here.

"The Amazing Archie Mills, is it really you? I haven't seen you in like... forever!'

Izzy jumps towards me, hugging tightly with all her might.

"Well, it sounds like you've had a lovely day, all the while I've been staring at my calculator and commiserating the loss of a promotion," growls Dad.

The bickering from the kitchen interrupts Izzy's hug.

"Wait! Are your mum and dad having an argument? They never argue? What are they arguing about, Archie?"

It's time to tell Izzy that I'm about to become a jet-setting globetrotter.

"Oh, nothing really, I think they're just having a heated conversation about me flying to America tomorrow."

Here's a tip for you, if you want to get someone's attention quickly, tell them you're flying to America first thing in the morning...

"HUH!"

"AMERICA?"

"WHAT!"

"WHY?"

"HOW?"

"WHEN?"

Yep, I had a feeling that's how she'd react.

I'm going to have to elaborate further.

"Well, it's no biggie really, I just have to go and perform on a little TV programme called *The Ella Show*," I calmly declare, whilst seriously underplaying the enormity of my current situation.

"*THE ELLA SHOW!*" yelps Izzy, now shaking with excitement. "My best friend is going to be on *The Ella*

*Show*! Ahhhhh!" Izzy screams while running round in circles like a dog chasing its tail.

"Ooh, ooh, can I come? I can pretend to be the yoga instructor who makes you all zen and calm before you go on stage."

"Nice try, Izzy, but right now judging by the conversation coming from the kitchen, I'm not sure If I'll even be going…"

After telling Izzy my good news, she marches us upstairs, shouting orders in the style of a military commander.

"Seven days means seven pairs of pants and seven pairs of socks, and you'll need spares just in case."

Pants, of course. I can't go to America without pants… Otherwise, they'll be calling me 'Captain No Pants."

Izzy is hunched over rifling through my pants drawers, launching my underwear over her shoulders.

"Your toothbrush — when people go on holidays, they always forget their toothbrush — grab it, quick!"

She's right, I can't go to America with furry teeth…

Izzy spins on her heels, stopping me.

"Oh, wait! What are you going to wear onto *The Ella Show*? You need something mega, something extravagant, something that says 'My name is Archie Mills and I have arrived'."

I don't think Izzy is going to believe that I now have a stylist, an agent and a whole team of people who get paid to look after me.

"OMG, you have a stylist called Fabio? And he's Italian? You do know the Italians dress the best, right, which means you're going to be a style icon."

Right now, that means nothing, because of all the clothes in all the world there's only one item that matters to me, and it's hung on my wardrobe door.

"OK, Izzy, before we start stuffing my suitcase full of pants, pants and more pants, let's make sure my jacket is tucked in there snug as a bug."

I reach for Blue's jacket, and as soon as my fingertips touch the fluffy purple fur, an electrical surge shoots right up my arm, tingling through my body. That warm and fuzzy unforgettable feeling has returned again and it feels magical.

Despite the sheer delight which I'm experiencing, I act coy and nonchalant as I gently place Blue's jacket into my suitcase, making sure Izzy doesn't make contact with it.

"Looks like someone's fallen in love with their purchase from Percy's," smiles Izzy.

Little does Izzy know, without this jacket, I wouldn't be going to America, I wouldn't have an agent and I wouldn't have won Wandsworth's Got Talent.

Just as we zip up my suitcase, Mum pops her head through my bedroom door.

"Izzy, darling, do you mind skedaddling on home, I need to have a little word with Archie."

"Sure thing, Mrs Mills," Izzy bounces from my bed and onto her feet.

When something BIG happens in our lives, Izzy and I do our secret celebratory handshake.

We do it when we're really excited, like last week when we travelled on the train all by ourselves. All best friends should have their own trademark, signature handshake. And this is ours…

**\*KNUCKLE\***
**\*KNUCKLE\***
**\*CLAP\***
**\*CLAP\***
**\*SLAP\***
**\*SLAP\***
**\*SPIN\***
**\*HIGH FIVE\***

Izzy leaves before shouting up the stairs, "See you on TV, mate."

**\*BANG\***

The front door slams behind Izzy. Mum sits on my bed, putting her hand on my lap.

"Archie, darling, I've just spoken to your father… He doesn't want you to go to America."

"WHAT! You can't be serious? But what about The Ella Show? Andy? My fans?"

Yep, this is what it feels like to have your hopes and dreams crushed into smithereens. Just a few days ago, I was a normal, everyday, typical kind of kid. Then, I miraculously find a magic jacket, discover I have a voice, win a talent competition and become popular overnight, and just like that it's all taken away from me in the blink of an eye.

Like a bucket with a hole in it, I now feel empty. The water in the bucket has been replaced with sadness. I'm an empty bucket full of sadness. That doesn't even make sense, nor does my dad's silly decision.

As my eyes well up, Mum's face begins to glow a shade lighter.

"Dad is just sad… He wants you to follow in his footsteps and become an accountant. I get it, I understand. That's Dad's dream. But Archie, my boy, you are an eagle, and you have to spread your wings and fly high, high into the sky. Dad can't clip your wings, especially when Mum's the boss. You have to dream your own dreams. Now, get your beauty sleep and count some sheep, because tomorrow, you're flying to America, and Dad will be there to wave you off."

I can't believe it; the bucket is now full and overflowing with joy. I'm a bucket full of happiness!

Mum sets my suitcase on the ground and tucks me into bed. She turns off my light and whispers before gently closing the bedroom door behind her.

"Tomorrow is going to be the first day of the rest of your life. Sweet dreams, my love."

**Dreams...**

**Sleep...**

**Sheep...**

***Zzzz...***

**Snoreeeee...**

# Chapter 15

***BING BONG***

"Ladies and gentlemen, this is a passenger service announcement, the nine a.m. Air America flight from London Heathrow to New York will soon be boarding from Gate 58," booms a voice over the airport tannoy.

This is it, never in my wildest dreams did I think I'd be flying to New York City to perform on *The Ella Show*. And here I am, standing in the middle of Heathrow airport about to get on a plane.

"*Ciao, ciao,* coming through, *amigos*!"

Fabio wheels into the airport with seven suitcases stacked high on a trolley.

"Mr Mills, how nice to see you, and Mrs Mills, looking radiant as ever."

Arriving in all his grandeur, Fabio, as always, is in full-on complementary mode this morning.

Mum nudges Dad. "Told you they were sweethearts, Harry."

Dad pipes up, "Wow, Fabio. Seven suitcases? Are you planning on immigrating to America?"

Fabio cackles and puffs out his chest, while proudly standing beside his collection of suitcases.

"No, no, no, Mr Mills. Our star needs outfits! Outfits and options. An option A, B, C, D, E, F, G… I could go on for the whole of the alphabet."

It looks like Fabio's brought enough garments to cloth the whole of New York.

And here comes Andy too.

"The Mills family and our man of the moment; morning, kid."

Andy pats me on the back before shaking Dad's hand.

"Congratulations, Mr Mills, your boy is the next best thing since sliced bread. You'll be able to retire soon."

Dad laughs, as Andy instantly turns on the charm.

"And don't worry, he's in safe hands. We'll look after your boy, Mr Mills."

***BING BONG***

"Gate 58 is now open for departure," sounds the airport flight announcer.

Mum squeezes me tightly and kisses me on the forehead. "Good luck, my darling boy, you're a star."

Dad throws his arm around me. "I'm sorry, Archie, sorry for being a pushy parent. It doesn't matter if you're an accountant or a singing sensation, I'll always love you, son. Go get 'em, tiger."

We wave goodbye and walk towards the check-in desk, leaving Mum and Dad standing at the front doors.

Mum is getting emotional, wiping a tear from her eye.

"Call us when you land," she shouts.

Fabio loads his seven suitcases onto the check-in desk conveyor belt, but there's only one case that matters. A special suitcase. My suitcase, the suitcase carrying Blue's jacket. I've even written '*FRAGILE*' down the side of the suitcase just to be safe... Hopefully, the baggage groundsmen are extra careful when putting it on the plane. I really do hope nothing happens to Blue's jacket.

"OK, kid, passport... check! First class ticket to New York... check! Well, it looks like we're all set, our bags are on and the plane awaits. The land of opportunity, here we come."

Andy beams and points his chin in the air, marching us towards Gate 58.

"New York, New York, so good they named it twice. In America, everything is bigger, better, faster and louder. You want a drink; they give you a gallon of the stuff. You want a hotdog; they give you a sausage the size of a submarine!"

By the sounds of things, I'll not be able to fit on the plane when I come back.

"The Big Apple, home of The Statue of Liberty, yellow taxis, giant slices of pepperoni pizza and, of course, *The Ella Show*... You're gonna love it, kid."

Despite being a little nervous, I'm incredibly excited, and it seems everybody else in the airport is excited too. Think of all these different people, going to different places to see different family and friends. To eat different types of food and listen to different styles of music. I wonder if any of them are going to *The Ella Show*?

We pass through Gate 58 and bounce down the gangway that connects the plane to the airport terminal.

*BOING*

*BOING*

*BOING*

"Good morning, sir, and welcome on board this Air America flight to New York."

The flight attendant is a happy American lady with the whitest teeth in the world. She scans our tickets without breaking her smile.

"First class, right this way." The attendant points to her left.

I've never been in first class before, I've only travelled in economy. Anytime we go on family excursions, we get the cheapest ticket; standard fare. Apparently, first class is for rich businessmen and women with lots of money... But how different can it really be?

HOLY MOLY!

IT'S DIFFERENT ALL RIGHT!

Instead of a normal plane seat, I get a giant reclining sofa that turns into a bed. There's a widescreen TV the size of a cinema screen. And a 'service' button that I can press when I'm hungry or thirsty.

"Sir, my name is Sandra and I'll be looking after you on today's flight."

Sandra is the happy smiley lady who welcomed us on the plane. She's dressed in a navy, white and red uniform; the colours of the American flag.

"Let me start you off with a complimentary hot towel to freshen your face, and here's a nice cold glass of American cola, and a bag of pretzels," offers Sandra.

I could get used to this; complimentary means free, and free is good!

My mum always told me, "If it's free, take it."

To my right, Andy sits with his face buried in a newspaper so big it must've taken half a forest to make it. He's chowing down green olives and drinking yellow fizzy bubbles from a crystal glass.

To my left, Fabio is cold out with his mouth wide open, catching flies. He's wearing a glittery eye mask that says '*Sleeping Beauty*'. Better not disturb him.

Well, it looks like I'm going to have to entertain myself for the next eight hours and 5585 kilometres of this journey from London to New York.

We'll be flying straight over the Atlantic Ocean with nothing below us but deep blue water, millions of fish and maybe a cruise liner or two.

Part of me feels bad… I'm up here drinking cola and eating pretzels while Blue's jacket is stuffed in the baggage hold under the plane. It must be freezing down there. Blue's jacket should be right here next to me… and so should Izzy… and Mum and Dad.

"Hey, kid, look who's on the list of movies on the inflight entertainment guide."

It's *Tommy and the Tiger*! I saw his poster at Andy's office!

"He's one of our clients… That's what happens when you work with Astounding Artists. Someday, you'll have an album on here too, kid."

I've never watched *Tommy and the Tiger*, but to have three movies in the 'Classics' section of this plane is just crazy.

I pop on my headphones and press play.

The screen turns black as the narrator's voice rumbles over the opening credits. "A long, long time ago, a legend roamed the land. A land ravaged by tigers. That legend was Tommy… Tommy the Tiger Tamer…"

# Chapter 16

"Hey, kid, wake up. You're missing the view."

"Hey, Archie, wakey, wakey!"

***SHAKE***

***SHAKE***

***SHAKE***

*What's going on?*

*Where are we?*

*And why is Andy shaking my shoulder?*

"Look, kid, the Statue of Liberty."

I did it again. I fell asleep. I've slept right through the entire flight, through *Tommy and the Tiger* 1, 2 and 3.

"And over there, that's the Empire State Building."

Andy is excitedly pointing out all the landmarks in New York's skyline as the plane glides through the air, slowly lowering in its descent. Golden sunlight pings off skyscrapers glistening in the distance. This is incredible, I've never seen a city so majestic.

"But the best of all has to be Central Park; ever seen a park so beautiful, Archie?"

Now I know why they call it The Big Apple; it really is green...

"Ladies and gentlemen, this is your captain speaking. We'll shortly be landing at JFK Airport. I want to thank you all for choosing to fly with Air America. We wish you a very pleasant stay and hope to see you again soon."

*SCREECHHHH*

The tyres slam onto the tarmac as the plane skids down the runway.

And just like that, Fabio is now awake too; Sleeping Beauty has slept.

Fabio unbuckles his seatbelt and bounces to his feet, hopping towards the exit door like an excitable kangaroo.

"Come, Archie, come, let's grab our bags and explore the city."

We scamper through first class towards the exit door where Sandra is standing, and still smiling.

"Welcome to America, guys, have a wonderful trip!"

*WOW!* I make my way to the exit door and it's like a scene from a movie. I'm standing on the top step of the plane stairwell and the sweet smell of America fills my nostrils. The heat gently warms my face. Andy was right, everything does seem bigger, better and brighter, even the air feels a little more electric. Skyscrapers fill the blue backdrop that sits in front of us.

"Breathe it all in, Archie kid… This is it, 'The Land of Opportunity'."

Andy is now standing alongside us.

"It really does get better each time I come," delights Andy.

I close my eyes and pinch my shoulders, taking a giant deep breath while filling my lungs. I want to remember this moment forever. My first time in America.

We clamber down the steps of the plane and whisk through the arrivals terminal towards baggage reclaim. Fabio is leading the charge.

"OK, so all we have to do is wait for our bags and then we're free to go crazy. I know the best pizza joint in all of New York City. It's on 5th Avenue, they do the most incredible strawberry milkshakes with cream and cherries on top. We'll go there straight after. Our bags should be here any minute now."

We stand at the side of the conveyor belt and wait patiently as we're joined by more people from our flight.

*TICK*
*TOCK*
*TICK*
*TOCK*
*TICK*
*TOCK*

These seem like very long minutes.

Bags and suitcases travel round the conveyor belt; big bags, small bags, wide bags and narrow bags, just not our bags. One by one, all of the people on our flight collect theirs, but there's no sign of ours...

"Our bags! Where are our bags?" demands Fabio.

As the clock ticks, more and more people leave the terminal and fewer bags remain on the conveyor belt.

Fabio is getting more agitated with every passing second, so Andy tries to find some answers at the airport help desk.

"Our clothes, our precious clothes, where are they?"

Fabio looks like he's about to cry... He's flailing his arms in the air and pacing back and forth.

We're now the only people left in the baggage reclaim.

All the other passengers on our flight have come and gone.

Andy comes back from the airport help desk and the expression on his face doesn't look good.

"Bad news, kid, our bags didn't make it onto the plane. Somehow, they've ended up on the wrong flight. They could be anywhere — Timbuktu, the Bermuda Triangle, the North Pole! Apparently, it takes seven days for them to show up, so we're just going to have to go and buy you some new clothes."

*Buy new clothes!*

*How an earth can you just go and buy a new magic jacket!*

Sure, we'll just pop out and buy a brand-new magic jacket, shall we? Like that's even possible, like you can replace the irreplaceable? 'Excuse me, ma'am, have you got any magic jackets lying around in the stockroom? Great, I'll have a size small, please; actually, give me five just in case I lose any in the future.'

"Noooooooo, why has this happened to us!"

Fabio falls to his knees, he's in floods of tears and I feel like joining him.

There's an old saying: 'what goes up, must come down', and right now, I feel like my rollercoaster ride has just crash-landed.

Without Blue's jacket, I haven't got a voice...

Without Blue's jacket, there's literally no point in us being here.

Is this the end of the road for Amazing Archie the Singing Sensation?

The end of the journey before it even began?

# Chapter 17

On the other side of the arrivals exit door, we're greeted by a sea of people from all around the world; Chinese, Indian, African, Australian — people of all shapes and sizes excitedly waiting to see who walks through the door next. But they're not waiting for me, these aren't my fans, do I even have fans in America?

"Archie Mills, pick up for Archie Mills!"

A big broad American man dressed in a black suit is holding a white sign with my name on it.

Hold on! This guy knows me! Is he a fan? He must be. Andy swoops in to introduce us.

"Hi, I'm Andy from Astounding Artists, you must be our chauffeur. This is Archie."

Our chauffeur? So he's not a fan, great...

"Pleased to meet you, Archie. My name's Marty and I'll be your limo driver for today."

Limo driver? I didn't know we were getting a limo. This is news to me.

Marty's demeanour is instantly comforting, his handshake lets me know that everything is going to be OK. Even though I've just found out Blue's jacket is now potentially lost forever, Marty's warm smile and friendly glow makes me feel ten times better. He's like hot chocolate on a cold winter's night.

"So you guys flew all the way from England with no luggage?" quips Marty.

Fabio's eyes begin to fill up, a stylists worst nightmare reimagined, but Andy quickly jumps in with an explanation as to why we're travelling so light.

"Well, we've had a little bit of a hiccup with our bags, heavens know where they are right now. But as they say in our industry, the show must go on!"

Marty pats me on the back with a reassuring hand.

"I'm sorry to hear that, buddy, but don't worry, New York is the home of shopping. We've got shopping malls the size of small cities. Plus, you're in New York, you don't need clothes to have a good time."

Maybe Marty's right, maybe I can still be a star without Blue's jacket...

Marty walks us into the airport car park.

"Have you ever ridden in a limo before, champ?" he asks.

"Not unless the bus counts... This will be a first for me."

"I've been driving people around for years, and if you're riding in the back of a limo, you must be doing something right in life. You know what I'm saying, pal?"

*BEEP*
*BEEP*

Marty hits a button on his keys and walks us towards the longest limo I've ever seen. Not only is it the longest, it's the shiniest. I can see my reflection in Marty's big black limo and right now my face doesn't look so sad.

"This is usually the part where I throw your bags in the boot, but you ain't got any, so hop in."

Marty hits another button on his key fob and the limo doors automatically slide open. The inside of the limo is just as jaw-dropping as the outside. It's the length of a bowling alley. We've got tinted windows, a drinks cabinet, heated seats that massage your bum and a jukebox with thousands of songs.

Marty starts the engine and revs the accelerator which roars like a lion.

*VROOM*

*VROOOM*

*VROOOOM*

"So you're staying at The Hand Hotel on 5th Avenue. You're going to love it there, bud; it really is something else."

It's funny how all it takes is one person to change how you feel, and right now that person is Marty.

If you think negative, then you'll feel bad, but if you think positive, you can only feel better. There's another saying; "always look on the bright side of life", and right now that's all we can do...

"Dude, have you ever ridden through Times Square with your head hung out the sunroof of a stretch limo? Well, today's your lucky day."

Suddenly, the giant TV screen on the roof starts to slide backwards, as sunlight and blue sky now fills the newly formed hole above us.

"Go ahead, jump up and suck it all in, bro. When you ride with Marty, you ride in style."

I climb onto my seat and poke my head through the sunroof, tightly clutching the edges of the limo with both hands. The air fills my mouth and pummels my cheeks.

"*COWABUNGA!* This is so cooooool!"

If you're going to scream at the top of your lungs, it may as well be out of a sunroof while riding in a limo through New York City.

Times Square is like a giant spaceship slapped bang in the middle of NYC. Thousands of billboards hang from the sides of buildings and multi-coloured strobe lights fizz through the air. Flashing adverts pop up on billboards illuminating the sky. People walk the pavements dressed as superheroes and yellow taxis whizz past, honking horns and skidding down side streets. The air smells like hot dogs and fried onions. It's a colosseum of energy.

"This is why they call it 'the city that never sleeps'. It's a living, breathing, beast; an amphitheatre of spirit and dreams."

Marty is now becoming more and more poetic, proud and patriotic with every sentence.

"And just to your left, The Hand Hotel. It's fit for a king, and every king needs a castle, and tonight that castle is yours, buddy old pal."

I'm looking up, and up, and up, up until my neck can't look up any more. I'm looking up so much it actually hurts to look up. The Hand Hotel is so tall it pokes out above the clouds. I bet it touches outer space.

"Here you go, bro, The Hand Hotel."

Marty's limo pulls onto the hotel forecourt. He turns round through the gap in the limo window that separates the driver's carriage from the passenger carriage, and offers me his hand.

"I hope you enjoy your stay in New York, Archie, and remember if you ever need anything, day or night, make sure to give me a call. A wise man once told me, 'if you have the power to make someone happy, do it'. The world needs happiness now more than ever."

"Thanks, Marty, you're a good guy. The world would be a better place with more people like you..."

# Chapter 18

Standing in front of this gigantic building has made me realise just how enormously my life has changed in a couple of days.

In little under a week, I've:

*Found and lost a magic jacket

*Won a talent competition and the thousand pounds top prize

*Been viewed more than ten million times online

*Appeared on the news

*Appeared in a magazine

*Travelled on the train on my own

*Turned down a job from the CEO of a multi-million-pound company

*Gotten an agent

*And, I've flown first class

I've done more in a week than some people will ever do in a lifetime, and it's only just begun. Amongst the craziness and hysteria of becoming an overnight success, I've completely forgotten about having to perform on *The Ella Show* tomorrow night.

In fact, I've completely forgotten about my old life. My family and friends. My house on 143 Oakhill Road. It's all a blur… one crazy, hazy blur.

But I haven't got time to dwell or be nostalgic, because a small man dressed like a penguin has just swivelled out of The Hand Hotel's revolving doors and he's fast approaching.

"Good evening, gentlemen, and welcome to The Hand Hotel. My name is Sebastien and I'll see you all inside. Please do let me know where your luggage is and I'll have the concierge bring it in."

Fabio's bottom lip begins to quiver once again.

Andy quickly changes the conversation to avoid any upset.

"Ah, Sebastien, an Englishman in New York. What's brought you all the way over here?" remarks Andy.

"Well, they do say the English are the elitists of good manners, which is why I was headhunted to look after the hotel's most prestigious guests. I've served everyone from the queen to the first man in space, and now I'm at your service, and the service of Amazing Archie the Singing Sensation. Please do follow, right this way, gentlemen."

Well, I've gotta say I thought Marty's manners were pretty darn good, and Pierre gives me free pastries, so I think the English have stiff competition. At least, from the Americans and the French.

Sebastien takes us through the hotel's main plaza which is decorated in marble from top to toe. There's marble floors, marble statues, marble plant pots, there's even a marble bridge crossing a river that runs right through the middle of the hotel.

Wait, there's an actual river running through the middle of our hotel? Yes, there is — and a gondola transporting guests to their rooms. Luckily for us, the gondola is made from wood, not marble.

We're next to board the small Italian-styled canal boat...

I imagine this is what Venice is like, if Venice was located inside a hotel.

"Listen, kid, we've got a pretty crazy day tomorrow. Fabio is going to hit the city and find you a new outfit for the big occasion, so I want you to kick back and relax. Recharge the batteries, order some room service, put your feet up, take a bath or watch cartoons. Do whatever it is that doesn't require energy because you need all the rest you can get before *The Ella Show*. I want our starman on top form."

Rest sounds good to me. I'll call Izzy, Mum and Dad when I get to the room, that doesn't require too much energy.

"All aboard now," shouts Sebastien.

We board the gondola and float down the river. Leafy            tropical trees on the banks of the river brush against us as we pass under the marble bridge.

"Just here please, this is Mr Mill's stop."

Sebastien halts the gondola operator.

"You'll be staying in our penthouse presidential suite, Mr Mills."

The presidential suite! But... I'm not a President!

"What did I tell you, kid; stick with Astounding Artists and you'll go far in life!" jokes Andy.

We hop off the gondola and enter the awaiting elevator. Another man dressed like a penguin stands inside, guarding the buttons of each floor. We shoot through the sky, rocketing upwards towards the 1001st floor. I didn't know it was possible to have so many floors in a building — that's a lot of steps if we break down. We're so high up, our ears pop just as we stop at the top.

**\*DING\***

The elevator opens to reveal a long narrow corridor with a single door at the other end.

It's the door to the 'the presidential suite'.

"Rest up, kid, I'm staying on the floor below, floor 1000. If you need anything, just give me a call. Order whatever you want to the room, it's all paid for. Enjoy your evening and get a good night's sleep, Archie."

Andy, Fabio, Sebastien and the other penguin disappear as I walk down the narrow corridor towards 'the presidential suite.'

The corridor has bright orange carpet, it's the colour of an African sunset. It's soft and springy, it has the feeling of a new carpet that hasn't been walked on much.

**\*SWOOSH\***

My room door has just slid right open. It must be electronic, motion censored, maybe it's facial recognition, I certainly didn't need keys to open it.

As I creep from the corridor into my room, I'm knocked for six and blown away by what's in front of my very eyes.

"WOOOAAAHHH!"

Look at this place, it's a palace...

There's a fish tank the length of the room housing multicoloured fish from around the world. A copper bath sitting in front of a giant glass window overlooking Central Park. A mini-arcade nestled in the corner with a pinball machine, pool table and a virtual racing car game. And the bed... I've never seen a bed like it. It's the size of a football pitch, I could run laps around it. The headboard is the height of a wall, and there must be fifty fluffy cushions to lay your head on. I wonder if any presidents have played the virtual racing game?

In movies, the first thing people do when they check into a hotel room is run and jump on the bed, and that's exactly what I'm going to do...

"Three, two, one... CANNONBALL!"

**\*UMPHH\***

I land on the bed and it feels like I've fallen onto a cloud. Man, this is comfy, I could lie here forever.

Maybe I'll rent a room here and make it my permanent residence. Like Marty said, I'm the king of the castle, but every king must have a queen... which reminds me, I need to ring Izzy.

The phone on my bedside table is an old, gold, antique phone with an L-shaped handle and a rotating spinning dial. I've never used one of these before. And to make things even trickier I'll have to use the international dialling code to call through to England.

I think the international dialling code is +44

Wahey, it works, it's ringing, I'm calling Izzy...

*RING RING*

*RING RING*

*RING RING*

Izzy's not answering; that's strange, she always answers her phone.

I guess I'll just send her a text.

Now is the perfect time to tell her about Blue's magic jacket saying it's potentially gone forever.

*'Hey Izzy, I've landed in New York. I'm staying at The Hand Hotel, in The Presidential Suite, 1001 floors up. It's so cool but I miss you and wish you could be here. Ooh and our luggage got lost on the flight out. I don't know where Blue's jacket is, which means I no longer have a voice, and I don't think I can perform on The Ella Show without a voice. Anyways, give me a call when you get my text and I'll explain more.*

*Love,*

*Archie X'*

I'll try mum and dad instead, they'll definitely answer. We're five hours behind London so they'll just be getting ready for bed.

I put in the international dialling code and spin the rotating dial a few more times and hey presto, it's working.

**\*RING RING\***
**\*RING RING\***
**\*RING RING\***

That's strange, Mum and Dad aren't answering either…

I wonder if something has happened to the phone network back in Wandsworth Town? Maybe a meteorite has struck London? I'm sure everything is fine… Maybe they're just busy.

If I just close my eyes and rest my head on these comfy, fluffy, cushions, I'm sure Mum and Dad will ring back and wake me up. And Izzy too.

I'll just close my eyes for a minute, and then I'll go and play the racing game, order some room service, have a bath and marvel out the giant window overlooking Central Park

Just another minute…

Sixty seconds of slumber.

A pick me up power nap.

There's no way I could snooze for any longer than a minute, after all I had forty winks and more on the plane ride here.

I sure am comfy…

Really comfy…

So comfy I could…

*Zzzzzzzzzz*

# Chapter 19

***BANG***
   ***BANG***
   ***BANG***

"Hello, room service," squeaks a strange, high-pitched voice from outside my bedroom door.

Uh oh, I've done it again. I've slept right through the night, like a bear deep in hibernation. I must've been out cold for fourteen hours straight. I'm not sure if it's jetlag or energy drain from wearing Blue's jacket but soon they'll be calling me Amazing Archie — The Sleeping Sensation... I don't even know what time it is.

I check my phone. It's twelve p.m. It's midday and I still haven't received a single text or a missed phone call from Mum, Dad or Izzy!

What's going on?

"*Ahem...* I said, ROOM SERVICE!"

The voice outside the door has now become a little impatient and less high-pitched.

But I didn't order room service, I've been sleeping the whole time, so who's at the door?

I hop off the bed and walk past the fish tank and...
***SWOOSH***

The electronic, motion-censored, mysteriously opening door slides ajar.

"Rise and shine, kid."

It's not room service at all; it's Andy and Fabio, and they look bright as buttons.

"Today's the biggest day of your life, which means you gotta eat like a king…"

Andy kindly hands me a trayful of beautifully smelling food. Fluffy American pancakes drizzled in maple syrup with shards of crispy bacon on top, a glass of freshly squeezed orange juice, with yogurt and fruit on the side too.

"You know what they say, 'breakfast is the most important meal of the day'. Well, you missed it, sleepyhead, so here's some brunch instead," smiles Andy.

This is quite the banquet.

I carry the tray to the table and chairs that sit next to the copper bath overlooking Central Park. Andy and Fabio follow as the mysteriously operating door slides behind them.

The floor-to-ceiling window of my room dramatically frames the epic panoramic picture that lies ahead. What a view. There must be twenty thousand trees in Central Park, of many different sizes and shades of green. I wonder how many species of trees there are. I'd say at least a hundred and fifty… Central Park really is a magnificent square of nature guarded by the goliath-like skyscrapers of New York's concrete jungle.

*I'll tell you what else is magnificent, these pancakes, mm mm mmm...*

"So, I've spoken to the producers of *The Ella Show*, and they want you to sing the song that you performed at Wandsworth's Got Talent. Exactly just how you did on the night you won the competition. Sound good, kid?" proposes Andy.

**\*GULP\***

How can I perform the way I did without a magic jacket? I won the competition not knowing what words were about to come out of my mouth. That's how powerful Blue's jacket is. I can't do it on my own, not without a magic jacket... I should just come clean and tell Andy I can't sing.

"My turn, my turn, my turn..."

Just as I put my knife and fork down to break the bad news, Fabio interrupts. He's been giddily bouncing on the spot since he entered the room, while holding a long black bag that's attached to a clothes hanger.

"OK! So when I left the hotel yesterday, I wanted to cry. Our outfits had disappeared like a puff of smoke, our precious, precious clothes. But in Italy, we have a saying *'Andrà tutto bene, vedrai!'* It means, 'Everything will be fine, you'll see!' So I picked myself up, put on my happy face and I went into New York City and found the outfit of the year"

Fabio slowly unzips the bag...

As the zip gets lower, and lower, and lower, I'm blinded by what's inside.

"Voilà!" exclaims Fabio.

A DIAMOND ENCRUSTED JUMPSUIT?

YOU'VE GOT TO BE KIDDING!

"Hand stitched by Leonardo the Great himself, Italy's most famous designer. He's a personal friend of mine and as it turns out, Leonardo is in town. So I borrowed it for your performance."

HUH!

Fabio has somehow managed to borrow diamonds?

Two hundred and fifty thousand dollars' worth of diamonds to be precise!

The price tag hangs from the jumpsuit. This is the pinnacle of absurdity. Blue's jacket cost twenty pounds from a second-hand store; this jumpsuit costs more than my mum and dad's house!

"As they say in France, this is the '*pièce de résistance*'." Fabio curtsies and ruffles his arms like a swan showing off its preened feathery wings.

"OK, Kid, enjoy your brunch, have a shower, get changed, then we'll all meet in the hotel lobby in an hour's time. Marty will take us to the TV studio."

Andy and Fabio exit, leaving me alone with the two hundred and fifty thousand dollar jumpsuit.

Well, I guess that's another first for me; I'm sitting in a room with a jumpsuit worth a quarter of a million.

Anyway, back to brunch, there's no time to be bowled over by diamonds and exuberance…

*NOM*

*NOM*

*NOM*

I don't know if it's because I'm hungry or nervous, but I demolish the pancakes in seconds.

OK, I need to shower, do my hair, try on this ultra-extravagant outfit and practice solo singing. Who knows, maybe I can sing without Blue's magic jacket…

People always say they're better singers in the shower, so if I'm going to practice anywhere, it may as well be in the shower.

I step inside the marble wet room which has the echoey reverb of a recording studio.

OK, the water is running, I'm standing under the giant waterfall-like showerhead, now all I have to do is sing… I'll just clear my throat and the words should just fly right out.

*Cough*

*Gargle*

*Splutter*

*Here we go… a one, two, a one, two, three, four…*

*"I'm the man,*

*Who walks…*

*And…*

*Talks…*

*I'm the man who walks, and talks and…"*

*DAMN! That wasn't very good. That wasn't very good at all.*

OK, maybe I'm just tense and stiff. When Izzy practices yoga, she normally loosens up beforehand. If I just shake my face, wiggle my arms and shimmy my hips, I should be more relaxed...

*"Look at me,*
*I'm as bright as can be...*
*I'm so darn bright,*
*I, I..."*

Can't sing right...

I can't sing, I just can't sing. I feel naked without Blue's jacket. I can't even string five words together, let alone a whole sentence or song. I'm going on live TV to perform in front of millions of people, and I can't even perform in front of the shampoo and conditioner.

To make things even worse, I still haven't heard from Izzy, Mum or Dad. They'd know what to do in this situation.

I haven't got a clue what to do.

I could just pretend to be sick? I could always say I've got a sore throat. I could mime. Fake singing! Yes, that's the answer! All pop stars do that nowadays. Miming and fake singing, that's the solution.

*\*RING RING\**
*\*RING RING\**
*\*RING RING\**
*AHHHH!*

I nearly jump out of my skin; the shower has a built-in phone. I thought it was a golden tap, it's actually a phone. How is it even possible to have a phone in the shower?

*Surely, this has to be Izzy, please be Izzy.*

I pick up what I thought was a tap and press it to my ear.

"Hey, kid, Marty's arrived earlier than expected; he's in the lobby waiting for us. Get your glad rags on and come join the party."

*What!*

*We're leaving and I'm not even ready!*

*PANIC MODE ENABLED!*

*SHUCKS, DOUBLE SHUCKS!*

*WHAT AM I GOING TO DO?*

*THIS CAN'T BE HAPPENING!*


*NO! ACTUAL NO!*

*GET A GRIP, ARCHIE!*

*Panic mode disabled!*

Looking in the bathroom mirror with sheer grit and determination, I give myself a pep talk.

"Come on, Archie, you can do this!"

As Fabio said, '*Andrà tutto bene, vedrai*!'; 'Everything will be fine, you'll see!' And it will be fine, it really will.

All I need to do is remain calm and breathe in… and breathe out. In… and out… You can do this, Archie. You've got this. Positive mental attitude!

It's working, I'm actually starting to feel calm.

If I try not to think about it, I guess everything might just work out fine. Who knows, this could be the best performance of my life.

I quickly pat myself dry, hop into my jumpsuit and style my hair. Before I know it, I've swooshed out my hotel room door, bounced down the corridor's orange springy carpet and plummeted 1001 floors downwards to The Hand Hotel's main foyer. And just like that, I'm on and off the gondola and walking through the front lobby where Marty's limo awaits.

"Afternoon, champ; you look like a million bucks."

"Well, a quarter of a million bucks to be precise, and a very good afternoon to you too, Marty." That's why I like Marty, I've only been with him three seconds and he's already made me feel better. And that's what you're supposed to do in life, pick people up and make them feel happy., especially when they're down. This positive mental attitude trick really is working.

I hop in the back of Marty's limo to join the rest of the gang.

"*Ciao, amigo*, you look *freddo*! Absolutely *freddo*!"

Fabio is bursting with joy. A tear runs down his cheek.

"That's why we employ him, kid. He's the best in the business. You look like a rockstar."

Gazing in awe, Andy and Fabio look at me like I'm a project they've just completed, like I'm a newly built house or a sunflower that they've nurtured     with tender love and care.

But in all the adoration comes the prowl and the growl of Marty's limo. Once again, he pumps on the accelerator.

*VROOM*

*VROOMM*

*VROOOMMM*

"Buckle up, boys, let's get you fine-looking gentlemen to *The Ella Show*."

*SCREEECCHH*

And we're off...

# Chapter 20

As we drive down 5th Avenue, I look outside and everything is in slow motion. The people rollerblading, the folk jogging, the shoppers shopping, even the dogs barking. There's a semi-naked guy playing the guitar wearing nothing but swimming trunks, a cowboy hat and cowboy boots, and even he seems to be in slow motion. Right now, everything outside Marty's limo is moving at a snail's pace, but my brain races at the speed of light.

I'm thinking about how this crazy journey started. Percy's Rags, Mr Mountgammy, what my classmates will think when the teacher asks "How was your summer holiday, Archie?" Will they even believe me? I'm not sure if I even believe myself.

Andy slides down the long limo sofa towards me and points out Marty's front window.

"There it is, kid. The Rockefeller Centre. Home of *The Ella Show*."

We're parked at the traffic lights a street away from the Rockefeller building which sits in front of us. It's within touching distance, but for some reason it seems like a million miles away.

"Once we cross this street, your life is going to change forever, kid… And who knows, you might even have some fans waiting outside."

FANS?

Andy winks at me, before sliding back to where he was originally sat.

What's Andy got up his sleeve?

As Marty's limo turns the corner, I find out exactly what's up Andy's sleeve…

**"*ARCHIE*"**

**"*ARCHIE*"**

**"*ARCHIE*"**

We're greeted by a wall of noise; a sea of fans have gathered outside the entrance of the TV studios.

Hundreds of boys and girls are chanting my name and holding up homemade banners.

"Looks like we've got company, kid," chuckles Andy.

The fans rush towards Marty's limo, banging on the windows and screaming my name. Camera lights flash through the tinted glass as the shouting gets louder and more deafening.

"We love you, Archie!"

*Did someone just say they love me?*

The limo is shaking from side to side like we're trapped in a human earthquake. Why are they shaking us? They're like zombies trying to break in. What's going on?

"Hey, Marty, honk your horn and scatter the crowd, then put your foot on the gas and drive straight through so security can let us in. We'll get eaten alive out here if we stay any longer." Even Andy seems a little anxious.

Marty slams his big, fat fist on the centre of the steering wheel.

*BEEP*

*BEEP*

The fans disperse backwards as Marty whizzes under a barrier manned by security guards.

We slip through an underground tunnel that leads us to an underground car park.

As we drive deeper into the car park, the screaming and chanting begins to disappear until we can't hear a thing. The noise has completely drained out.

Marty switches off his engine. *Phew, looks like we're safe.*

Just as I think the coast is clear, the limo door yanks open.

*AHHH, have one of the zombies escaped through security?*

"Howdy, y'all, and welcome to *The Ella Show*. My name's Kaycee and I'm going to be looking after y'all today."

Thank goodness, this guy works here, he's not a zombie.

"I see you met your fans, Archie! Ella posted a clip of you on her social media earlier today. I guess they love you just as much as we do. They've been standing outside all afternoon waiting for you... Anyways, let me take y'all right through to your dressing room."

Kaycee has a long, drawn-out southern American accent, he reminds me of a character from an old spaghetti western. He's tall and confident, dressed in black and walks with swagger. His boots have shiny silver buckles on the heels that make a funny clicking noise on every footstep. Kaycee is chewing gum and tilting his cap at each person we pass.

The corridors are full of people running around with lights, cameras, clipboards, props and trays of coffee. There's way more staff here than there was at *Live in London*. This place is like *Live in London's* older, bigger brother. The grown-up one. The one who makes all the money.

"Let's detour and quickly swing by Ella's dressing room and I'll introduce y'all before you go on stage."

Kaycee stops at a sparkly pink     door, giving it a rattle.

*KNOCK*
*KNOCK*
*KNOCK*

"Hey, Ella, I've got some visitors all the way from London who want to come and say hello," Kaycee shouts while pressing his head against Ella's door.

There's a crash, bang, clatter and a thud, and then the sound of heels running from the other side of the door towards us. The door flies open to reveal the most popular TV presenter in all of America.

"Archieeee baby, so good to see you!"

Ella throws her arms around my shoulders, planting a sloppy kiss on my cheek.

"Thank you soooo much for flying over here to perform on our little old show. We're so excited to have you."

Ella is actually thanking me for being here. She's genuinely happy to see me...

My cheeks are glowing, I've gone all rosy.

"It's my pleasure; in fact, I should be thanking you for inviting me here," I calmly reply.

"Shoot, I gotta go over my script and rehearse one more time before we go on air, but I'll see you on the studio floor, superstar."

*MWAH*

Ella plants another sloppy kiss on my cheek before turning round.

"Oh, by the way, I love your outfit; you look like a giant disco ball."

Fabio's head pops up like a meerkat... A very happy-looking meerkat, might I add. Not many meerkats receive such compliments from the queen of American TV.

"Why thank you, your highness of gorgeousness." Fabio curtsies one more time, again ruffling his arms like a swan showing off its wings.

Ella's door closes shut.

Well, that sure was exciting, almost as exciting as the journey to my dressing room.

We press on before stopping at a door with a golden star on it. In the middle of the star is my name, 'Archie Mills'. Ever since I met Andy, he's been telling me I'd be a star, and now I have a star on my dressing room door. In New York City. At *The Ella Show*. *Is this even real life?*

"Here we are, your very own dressing room." Kaycee pauses at the door.

"I'm going to take Andy and Fabio to the green room while you relax. Although, I should warn you, there's a little surprise waiting for you inside… C'mon, y'all, let's grab some donuts and bring you to the green room."

Kaycee whisks Andy and Fabio away, leaving me standing outside my door alone.

A surprise, what could it be? A puppy? A signed photo of Ella?

*Wait, maybe it's Blue's jacket! Please let it be Blue's jacket, is this the moment where I'm finally reunited with my most treasured possession…*

I take a deep breath, gently putting my hand on the doorknob, turning the handle slowly, to find…

"Archieeeeeeeeeeee!"

GREAT BALLS OF FIRE, IT'S IZZY!

IZZY IS HERE IN NEW YORK!

She leaps into my arms, latching onto me like a sloth hugging a tree.

"What on earth are you doing here? I tried to call you, I tried to message you and got no reply. I thought you were ignoring me!"

Izzy laughs as if it's all been one giant misunderstanding. "No, silly, I was flying over the Atlantic Ocean to come and see you. I had no phone signal and we wanted it to be a surprise."

We? Why is she saying 'we'?

"Did you actually think I was going to let my best friend go on American TV and not be here to support and cheer him on?" professes Izzy.

"You mean to say you flew to New York all by yourself?" I enquire suspiciously.

"No, silly, your mum and dad are here too. They're in the green room stuffing their faces. When Mr Mountgammy found out you were performing on *The Ella Show*, he gave your dad two weeks off and paid for our flights out."

WOWZER!

What a generous act of kindness; Mr Mountgammy is a nice guy too.

It's so nice to see Izzy, but it's time for the fairy tale to end.

133

I have to confess…

"I'm so glad you've come, Izzy, because I can't do it. I can't sing. I lost Blue's jacket and without it, I'm just a normal kid from Wandsworth Town. I have no voice… I've never had a voice. The jacket gave me superpowers. I'm a phony, a fake… I like maths and numbers and football, Izzy, I'm not a singer who performs on live TV. There's no way I could win a talent competition without a magic jacket. I'm just going to have to confess and tell Andy, Ella and the producers that I can no longer do the show. I'm so sorry you've come all this way for me to let you down."

I swallow what feels like my pride, as a massive lump, wedges itself between my throat.

"Wow, wow, wow, reverse your emotions, cowboy!" Izzy springs to life as if possessed.

"Archie, can't you see? You can do anything. Anything    in this world is    possible! You don't need a magic jacket, cloak or cape. The magic isn't inside Blue's jacket, it's in you. You can be an astronaut, a football player, you can be anything your heart desires… as long as you BELIEVE in yourself! That's all you gotta do. And when you believe in yourself, great things happen. Stardust, Archie! Remember, it's on your fingertips, on the tip of your tongue and it's coursing through your veins. You are a star and you will perform tonight as AMAZING ARCHIE THE SINGING SENSATION!"

Izzy's hands are tightly squeezing my shoulders, like an eagle clutching its prey. She's out of breath. That pep talk has taken the wind right out of her sails. She's staring me dead in the eyes, glaring into my soul. I've never seen Izzy look so serious, so animated, so alive! The concentration in her eyes is so intense, I can even hear her heart pounding against her chest as the breath rifles through her nostrils.

There's nothing but silence filling my dressing room, until...

*BANG*

*BANG*

*BANG*

"It's showtime, baby, we're about to go live!"

Kaycee's head pops through my dressing room door, breaking the intensity that Izzy and I find ourselves in.

This is it!

IT'S TIME!

TIME TO BELIEVE IN MYSELF...

IT'S TIME TO SHINE!

# Chapter 21

"Ladies and gentlemen, live from New York City, all the way from the Rockefeller Centre, it's your house band with the theme tune, Discoooobeard," the stage announcer bellows across the studio.

Discobeard kick into the theme tune, playing it with vigour and high-octane energy.

*Ting ting ting ta ta ta ta ting*
*Ting ting ting ta ta ta ta ting*

"The Queen of TV!"

"The best you've ever seen!"

"It's *The Ella Show*!"

"On your TV screen."

"And now for your hostess with the mostess, everybody's favourite chat show presenter; Rockefeller, raise the roof for Ellaaaaa!"

Ella walks on stage and the crowd go boogaloo, wailing in an excitable frenzy.

**\*YEYYYYY!\***

**\*WAHEY!\***

**\*WOOHOO!\***

They're clapping, smiling, whooping and hollering as Ella makes her way to the middle of the studio floor.

Bright studio lighting shines down on Ella, she looks like a goddess, with her sleek black hair and dazzling red dress. What a start to the show, the intro has been as much of a spectacle as the opening ceremony at the Olympics.

"Thank you, thank you, you're too kind, honestly! What a wonderful audience we have in tonight, and what a wonderful show we have in store for you guys."

It feels like I'm watching from home — but I'm not; I'm backstage peeking through a tiny gap in the curtains. This is the most surreal, bizarre experience of my life. I'm going to be on live TV in about thirty seconds.

Through the gap of the curtains, I can see Izzy, Mum, Dad, Andy and Fabio who're all sat in the front row, right next to Ella.

"Guys, please show your appreciation one more time for my awesome house band, Discobeard."

The crowd applauds one more time with mass appreciation.

Discobeard play every night of the week, Monday to Friday, performing the intro music and songs during the ad breaks. They're nearly as famous as Ella herself. Rossy is on guitar and vocals and Gary is on drums. Their trademark wacky Hawaiian shirts, shaggy hair and bushy beards occupy     the left-hand corner of the TV studio.

Ella walks to the brown mahogany desk where she presents the show from, plonking herself on a chair in front of a live image of Manhattan's skyline. I can see all the buildings we flew over when we first arrived; the Empire State Building, the Chrysler Building       and One World Trade Centre. And right next to Ella is the sofa where all the guests sit, where I'll be sitting in a moment's time…

"Now, my first guest comes from the country that gave us The Beatles, Buckingham Palace and fish 'n' chips. He's the latest internet star to go viral and he's flown all the way from London, England, to be here tonight. Please give a big, warm American welcome to Amazing Archie the Singing Sensation."

Kaycee pulls back the studio curtain and gives me the nod to walk on stage. I'm about to walk out to three hundred and thirty million people watching live from home. No pressure, no pressure at all, just don't trip. Here we go…

   **\*ARCHIE\***
   **\*ARCHIE\***
   **\*ARCHIE\***

Deary me, these Americans sure do like a chant. They're like the English but louder, ten times louder. Gosh, they really are going for it, fist pumping the air with sheer enthusiasm. This is a hero's welcome!

Ella greets me at the sofa with more kisses, one for each cheek.

"Amazing Archie the Singing Sensation, welcome to *The Ella Show* and welcome to the United States."

The crowd goes wild again, cheering as Ella and I take our seats.

"It's your first time here but it feels like we've known you for a lot longer — let's cross live now to our cameras outside the TV Studios. As you can see, 'Archie-Mania' has swept across New York City. Say hello to your new fan club, Archie."

*YIKES!*

The number of people now outside the TV Studio has more than quadrupled. There's a queue of boys and girls stretching right around the block. Not just boys and girls, someone's granny is wearing a t-shirt with my face on it.

"Have you got a message for your fans?" gestures Ella.

"Thanks for coming out, folks! You've no idea how special I feel right now. I didn't think people in my hometown knew me, let alone you lovely lot in New York City."

Wow, I actually can't believe this! Is this a dream?

"I have to say, Archie; you look fantastic, check out that jumpsuit. You're like a walking talking jewellery store with all those diamonds. So tell me, how does it feel to be famous?" Ella's eyes light up with the introduction of her first question.

"How does it feel? Weird! Really weird! A week ago, I was an average, everyday kinda kid. Now people have t-shirts with my face on them."

I begin to laugh at the absurdity of my current situation.

"And with good reason... On Saturday night, you won Wandsworth's Got Talent and now you're in New York, baby. You don't hang about! So what's the secret to your success? Years of hard work or magic?"

Ella laughs before sitting back to relax with one arm slouched over the side of her chair.

This is the moment that's going to make or break me...

It's time to tell the truth.

"Well, it's funny you should say that! I can't actually sing! But on Friday, the day before the talent contest, I bought a jacket with my best friend Izzy. A second-hand jacket from a thrift shop in Borough Market. It wasn't just any old jacket — little did I know, it was a magic jacket. It actually belonged to an American, a 1960s soul singer called Blue Davies who performed out here in Las Vegas. I guess Blue's magic never left the jacket and the next person to wear it would inherit his stardust. That was me. When I wore it, it gave me a voice. I could sing. Anyways, that's old news now, we lost the jacket on the flight out here. It could be anywhere right now... So it looks like next week I'll just go back to being plain old me. I can't sing without that jacket…"

*Ahhhhhhhhhhh!*

The audience gasps! Andy looks like his whole world has just collapsed around him. Izzy is shaking her head in disbelief. Fabio is covering his face with both his hands. And Ella just looks really, really sad.

"You lost your jacket? Your treasured magic jacket? Which means you can't sing any more? I feel awful. It's all our fault. I'm so sorry, Archie."

Ella's bottom lip begins to tremble.

The TV studio goes completely silent. The audience are on the edge of their seats waiting for my next words. Waiting for me to break the ice.

You could hear a pin drop.

I guess this is it, the dream is over…

"What if you had the world's greatest TV band playing alongside you?"

Gary from Discobeard rises from his drum stool.

"And what if I was on backup vocals and helped with harmonies?"

Rossy stands up too.

"And what if everyone in this TV studio got on their feet right now and told you 'you can do it', because you can do it, Archie. YES! YOU! CAN!"

Izzy is now on her feet too…

"Remember what I told you, Archie, the magic isn't in Blue's jacket, it's in you."

Ella stands up next and like a train of falling dominoes, the entire audience follows suit, the sound of seats flipping backwards ripples through the studio, as a slow clap begins. Everyone is on their feet, including Mum and Dad.

**"YES, YOU CAN!"**
**"YES, YOU CAN!"**
**"YES, YOU CAN!"**

Gary bangs his kick drum playing a beat over the chant. Rossy raises his arms in the air conducting the congregation to sing louder and clap faster. The rhythm of the instruments and the voices together is anthemic. Ella whispers in my ear, "Yes! You! Can! Honey!" while nodding to the microphone that stands in the middle of the studio floor.

It's my microphone. It's my moment. This is my time. I haven't flown thousands of miles around the world not to give it a go!

Rossy hushes the crowd, instructing them to lower their voices as the clapping drowns out.

I look at Dad and he silently mimes the same words as everyone else 'YES, YOU CAN...'

Right now, it's just me standing under a spotlight, in the middle of an American TV studio on live TV.

But can I?

The spotlight feels like a beam shining down from outer space. Like aliens in a UFO are transmitting some kind of powerful energy through my body.

I'm starting to feel something...

*OH BOY!*

*OUCH!*

*It's happening again...*

My toes are tingling. My ankles are shaking. My knees are wobbling. My pelvis is thrusting and my calves are fizzing. My shoulders are shimmying and my arms are cocking. My hands are pulsating and gravitating towards the mic stand.

This is it, I'm about to sing, but I can't do this alone.

"Hey, Gary, why don't you count me in with a beat..."

I've found my voice...

"My pleasure, Archie. A one, two, three, four."

***BA DUM DUM TISS****

***BA DUM DUM TISS****

***BA DUM DUM TISS****

***BA DUM DUM TISS****

Rossy swoops in with a stinging guitar solo.

**Ting ting ta ta ta ting***

**Ting ting ta ta ta ting***

**Zing zing za za za zing***

**Ting ting ta ta ta ting***

**Zing zing za za za zing***

**Ting ting ta ta ta ting***

Now it's my time...

Time to shine, Archie!

All eyes are on me.

HERE WE GO!

*"Now here's a story about a boy named Blue*
*An ordinary kid like me and you,*
*He liked to have fun but he worked real hard,*
*He knew the harder he worked, would make him a*
*star*
*So every day he tried*
*And to his surprise,*
*It's true…*
*If you work, work, work a little harder,*
*You'll be fast, quick and a little sharper,*
*You'll be big, clever and a little smarter,*
*If you work, work, work a little harder,*
*Just give it your best,*
*And you'll start to feel blessed*
*It's true…*
*It's trueeee…*
*It's trueeeeeeeeee…*
*It's trueeeeeeeeeeeeeeee…"*

I finish the last line and for the second time in as many days I receive a standing ovation.

Izzy runs on set jumping onto me like a baby monkey clutching its parent. Mum and Dad follow, and before I know it, I'm in my very own scrum with Rossy, Gary, Ella, Mum, Dad and Izzy.

I'm swept up in a sea of hugging arms and smiling faces as a wave of appreciation ripples through the TV studio with the audience and production staff whistling and cheering me on.

Uh Oh, what's happening?

Gary grabs under my armpits and Rossy is holding onto my legs, and that's Ella, Mum, Dad and Izzy's hands sliding under my back too, I have a feeling they're going to flip me like a pancake and give me the bumps

*GULP*

"3, 2, 1" signals Rossy with a look of menace across his face,

*Ahhhhhh*

They toss me skywards towards the studio lights.

*Woosh*

*Woooosh*

*Wooooosh*

I'm flying,

Soaring like a bird,

Buzzing like a bee,

Floating up like a butterfly,

My arms and legs are swirling in the air,

And, I'm plummeting back down to earth again.

*Woooosh*

They catch and propell me right back up again in one fell swoop, this time so high I nearly brush my nose against the zingy bright yellow studio light bulbs.

Thankfully on my descent back to earth, Rossy, Gary, Ella, Mum, Dad and Izzy catch me, gently cushioning my fall, but they're not letting go. I'm still floating in amongst their cloud of arms and hands.

"You know, you only truly become a rock and roll star after your first official crowd surf" shouts Rossy with bravado.

"Hey, how would you guys like to pass Amazing Archie the Singing Sensation over your heads?" chips in Gary, equalling Rossy's gusto.

*Waahhheyyyyyy*

Answers my new American fans, as I'm raised up by my very own family and friends' forklift, and passed like a parcel from the studio floor into the audience. They chant my name even louder as I hover above their heads.

I close my eyes just like I did when stepping out onto the stairwell when our plane first touched down in New York City, I'll never forget this moment.

The stardust and magic truly    has been inside me all along...

# Chapter 22

Well... New York really was a crazy adventure, a once-in-a-lifetime unforgettable trip that I'll savour forever.

Apparently, it was the most watched episode in the history of *The Ella Show*.

The President of the United States even sent me a letter. He called me an 'inspiration' and invited me to The Whitehouse on my return back to America

I guess I've learnt a lot from my trip away; but most importantly, I've learned to always believe in myself and to never give up.

I've seen things I never imagined seeing....

I've also made lots of new friends on the way...

Ella, Kaycee, Marty, Sebastien, Phoebe the photographer, Melissa and Dorothy McCarthy, Sandra the kind airhostess, Mr Mountgammy, Fabio, Andy and Kaya too.

But no matter how many new friends I make, I've realised the importance of cherishing my own dear family and inner circle.

They will always be there for you, no matter what you want to be in life.

When life gets hard, they'll always have your back...

I also realised there's no place like home, and no matter how famous or successful you become in life, you should never forget where you come from.

My name is Archie Mills and I come from Wandsworth Town, and I'm darn proud of it.

There truly is no place like home...

So what's next for Amazing Archie the Singing Sensation?

An album? A stadium tour? A job at Mountgammy Money Limited?

I don't know...

But one thing I do know is I'm taking the next week off from life.

It's time to slam on the breaks of this crazy out of control rollercoaster ride and kick back and relax for a minute or two.

I'm staying right here in Wandsworth Town and eating all the pastry Pierre can throw at me, at least that's my plan anyway.

As the taxi takes us on the final leg of our journey home, I start to get a little sentimental.

I've been in a limo in Times Square, I've looked over Central Park from a thousand and one floors up, but right now, Wandsworth Town is the only place where I want to be...

The taxi pulls up to our house; 143 Oakhill Road. I sure have missed you...

Just as Mum, Dad, Izzy and I get to the front door, my phone starts to ring. It's Andy.

What could he possibly want?

Another TV Show?

A performance for the queen of England?

I answer with intrigue.

And never did I ever expect to hear the next set of words...

"Hey, kid, good news..." shouts Andy. "They found your suitcase!"

# THE END